CATCHING THE DRIFT

AN ANGLER'S JOURNEY TO DIVINE

CATCHING THE DRIFT

AN ANGLER'S JOURNEY TO DIVINE

MATTHEW GUTCHESS

(aka, The Awakening Angler)

DEDICATION

I dedicate this book to my Grandparents Bill & Jean.
I live every day to honor your memory and to spread
the love to others that you always gave me.

Most importantly I would like to thank the love of my life,
my best friend, my partner and my fiancé Courtney Jean.
Without you, my love, this book stays just a dream.

I love you with all my heart!

PROLOGUE

The little Mexican restaurant that was right outside the back gate of the post was a familiar place to Jack, who removed his lid when he entered the tiny dining room. Rosey greeted him with the same smile from behind the counter as she always had and pointed toward the table at the back corner of the room.

"Do you want your usual to drink, señor?"

"Yes ma'am," Jack said, as he returned her smile.

The room was full of sound and smells as all ten tables were filled with soldiers having lunch on a beautiful mid-summer "Taco Tuesday." He heard bits and pieces of conversations as he walked to the back corner, much like he would in the mess hall. Upon arrival at the table he was greeted by a friendly face.

"Afternoon, Colonel," Jack extended his right hand for a shake.

"Hey, short-timer, great to see you; have a seat." Colonel Ortiz laughed. "It's hard to believe, Jack, that this will be our last lunch together after almost ten years. I always assumed our last meeting would be at one of the other's funeral after being blown up in some shit hole country we were trying to save."

"Well, sir, I see you're just a ray of sunshine today as always," he said, as he shook his head and took a seat. "If I decide to stay in the area, *maybe* we can continue our Taco Tuesday strategy meetings? After all, salmon season is right around the corner and we need to prepare."

"Wait, hold on a moment soldier, you mean to tell me that you are less than thirty days out from retirement, and you don't have a plan yet for what you're going to do or where you're going to go after Uncle Sam tells you goodbye? You're joking right?" Colonel Ortiz stared at Jack in disbelief.

"I'll have it all worked out by then, Sir. I've been so wrapped up in this last training cycle that this whole retirement thing has crept up on me."

"Crept up, or crept in? You know, Jack, no one is pushing you out the door. You're as good a soldier as I have ever served with, and an even better fisherman I might add. You've taken everyone from new privates to commanding generals out on the water in every location you've ever been stationed like you were a local born and raised guide. If you want to stay, you certainly can; you have enough high-ranking friends to change anything you want. Paperwork can be halted with one phone call by any one of them."

"Thank you, Sir, for that offer, really, but I'm not staying any longer. I may not be completely sure where I'm going yet or what I'm going to do, but it is time to do something else, that much I am sure of."

"I understand completely." Colonel Ortiz smiled at Jack and patted him on the shoulder, and with that out of the way the two men enjoyed their lunches and talked of past fishing trips and fond memories. As they parted ways in the parking lot afterwards, the Colonel told Jack, "I'll see you at the retirement ceremony and at the party following in the NCO club."

"What party? There's no party, Sir, I don't want a party!"

"It's already done and planned, Jack." And with a wave of his hand out the car window Colonel Ortiz drove away.

Two weeks passed in a blink and the day was upon Jack. The finality of the moment was far more emotional than he ever could have expected. Everywhere he went, soldiers were shaking his hand like he was already gone and jokingly calling him short-timer like he had won the lottery. All he could feel inside was unrest though, nagging uncertainty as to whether he was making the right decision. He smiled outwardly but couldn't help feeling like it was a funeral instead of a celebration. After today they would all go on without him, and soon enough he would be forgotten like he never existed at all. That was the last thought he had as he stepped out of formation after being called up front by Colonel Ortiz to start the ceremony.

"We are here today to honor and celebrate the contributions and the career of the finest soldier I have ever served with. He has given more to the United States Army than..."

The words trailed off in Jack's ears like someone had turned the sound all the way down and then off. He blankly stared at the battalion of faces standing in formation remembering how many times he had been on the other side of these ceremonies, never once imagining what it would be like when it was for him.

The speeches finally stopped, and the long line of hand shaking had begun. Jack was out of body and remembered very little of the small talk that took place during it. Before long, the crowd dispersed, and he returned to his barracks room to change out of his uniform for the last time before he was to be at the NCO club at seven. When he opened the door, he was greeted by a wagging tail and a wet nose on his hand, they belonged to Phineas Straw, aka, Fin, his ten-year-old black lab.

The room was empty except for a pile of tackle boxes and fishing rod cases, a rucksack, suitcase, and a few other miscellaneous things. The space was stark and devoid of any sign of life now even though Jack had spent the last ten years in this room.

It was Friday night and the clamor of sounds in the barracks below him signaled release for the troops and the excitement of a summer weekend off duty. Jack changed his clothes and started taking his belongings out to the parking lot to load in his truck. When everything was packed, including the dog, he left the key in the door and drove across base to the party in his honor.

The party droned on for Jack amidst stories, toasts, and speeches about what he had done and whom he had done it with, each one sounding more and more like a eulogy instead of a celebration. Jack laughed on the outside along with the crowd, but he was acutely aware of the fact that he was alone amongst them and that these same stories would continue whether he was physically there or not. The finality of the moment put his life in perspective. The Army had been like the parents he had never had, teaching him how to act, guiding him, and giving him the structure in life he subconsciously craved.

He had spent his life up until this moment hiding out inside its walls for security and a sense of belonging that was noticeably absent everywhere else, and now he stood firmly on the fork in the road looking for insight into which direction to go. He had no parents to go home and visit while trying to re-group. His mother, though still alive, was a distant entanglement of selfishness and guilt that he had long ago cut free from himself like a cancerous tumor. His father was a ghost who looked like a question mark. There was no other family that he had seen or spoken to since before he was a teen, thirty years removed from now. His grandparents were truly all he had, and they had been gone for twenty years.

The raucous laughter and a bellowing voice assembling all parties to the bar for another celebratory shot of some distilled spirit snapped Jack back to the present. He instantly feigned over-indulgence and the need to grab some fresh air as an excuse to get out of it. Amid taunts to the contrary, he assured the mob that he would return for the next round as he slipped through the crowd toward the door.

Slithering through the crowd like a serpent his progress was thwarted by a firm hand on his bicep which halted him and caused him to turn back. He saw Sgt. Nitz smiling at him as he was drawn closer for a one-armed hug and a congratulatory pat on the back.

"I've seen you slip out of places many times Jack, so I wanted to catch you before you were gone for good to give you your retirement gift."

"Thank you, Mike, that's very kind of you, I would have said goodbye though before I left."

"Bullshit you would've; I would have gotten a text six months from now asking how the new training cycle was going."

"We've been friend's a long time; you know me well."

"Yes, I do, so this is for you," as he stuffs the envelope into Jack's shirt, "I'm going to the bar, I'll see you around, buddy."

The summer evening was perfect as he escaped into it. The sun was three-quarters high and looked like a brightly glowing basketball in slow motion on its downward arc toward the hoop as the earth pulled it ever westward. Standing in the entrance, staring at the sun as it continued on its path, the door closed behind Jack and thus ended his military career. He was not going back in that room, he was not going to go through the litany of goodbyes, he was going to continue on his path, whatever that may be.

Crossing the parking lot to his truck he opened the door to a greeting from his oldest and dearest friend. Fin gave Jack a lick on the right ear to say hello as he sat in the driver's seat. "Let's go fishing before it gets dark down at our spot on the river."

The Black River got its name from the coffee-colored tannic waters that flow inside its banks. Its origins were in the old growth forests of the west slope of the Adirondack mountains. As it flowed westward toward Lake Ontario, it passed through the military base Jack had called home for ten plus years. He pulled into the little park where he often came after last formation to make a few casts and mentally digest his day one last time.

He looked at the card he had just been given lying on the dashboard and decided to open it. The outside said, "Congratulations on your retirement," inside was blank except for a hand-written note from his long-time friend.

"Sarge, I hear these are what civilians use to help them relax and enjoy themselves. God knows a tight ass, by the books, son of a bitch like you sure needs to relax and enjoy. Be well my friend. Mike."

Jack looked down in his lap and there having fallen out of the inside of the card were six perfectly rolled joints. He laughed out loud at the gift and the card and thought back to the days when him and his buddies would skip class in high school and get stoned and go fishing. Those were fond memories from a lifetime ago. Jack tucked the gift away under the seat as he looked over the river where he was about to go fishing.

The dock paralleled the water and there was a permanent bench in the middle where Jack set his tackle box while he was fishing if no one was around, which there rarely was in the evenings. He started to cast as Fin wandered about. Jack's mind did the same. The combination of drink and dreams swirling inside of him made a cocktail of euphoria and numbness. He could not focus clearly on hope or fear; he was even having a hard time focusing on the act of casting his rod, something that he had done countless times prior.

With repetition, the casts improved, and strangely he found himself thinking about the question mark that was the father he never knew. The thoughts of him danced through his mind like the flickering flames of a campfire. Who was he, what did he look like, where was he now? Wouldn't it have been special if he had him to return home to after his career serving his country, wouldn't that have made him proud? As the last words of that sentence trickled through his mind, he felt a strange tingle inside that felt like a chill, noticeably out of place in the hot and humid evening air of summer.

As the next cast flew from his rod, arcing across time and space before it hit the water with a splash, a single sentence inadvertently slipped off Jack's tongue and out into the universe: "**Who is my father**?"

The slip was met with surprise from Jack, as he had asked that question a million times before in his head but never once out loud. He instantly realized that saying it aloud felt different in some unexplainable way.

The cast had landed, the bail on the reel had been closed, and Jack was retrieving the lure, paying it no mind as he focused solely on what he had just said and how it made him feel. Suddenly, violently, and without warning, the rod was almost ripped from his hand like the lure was hooked to the bumper of a truck going in the other direction at eighty miles per hour.

The jolt hammered Jack's occupied mind like an uppercut from a heavyweight boxer, and his right arm slammed back instinctively in a hook set to meet the fish with equal force and securely lodge the hook deep into its jaw. The bass jumped free of the water nearly three feet in the air, twisting and glistening, using all of its strength to free itself from its captor. The splash of re-entry was met with an all-out dash to the bottom as the battle between man and fish raged in this peaceful little stretch of river.

Jack's senses were instantly on hyper-alert and adrenaline flowed through his veins as pinpoint focus was applied to the task at hand. As the seconds ticked away, Jack found himself glancing toward the bench where his tackle box sat. His eyes continued to steal glances every couple of seconds, and he was powerless to control them. Each time he looked, he saw the unmoving box sitting exactly where he had placed it. There was no change, and he could not understand why he continued to keep looking over at it.

The battle with the fish finally waned. Jack went down to one knee on the dock holding his rod high with his left hand, grabbed the bass by the lip with his right hand, and secured his catch for inspection, still on one knee, his torso upright as he held the perfect specimen. The fish now hung in his line of sight between him and his tacklebox.

The question mark of his father raced back into his mind like a soaking wet and muddy dog rampaging into a white-carpeted living room to shake off. Jack was aware that the thought and its timing seem odd. Shaking his head as if to clear internal cobwebs away, Jack's eyes returned to the fish but something beyond it moved and snared his attention as his eyes focused.

There on the bench, sitting side by side, smiling at him, holding hands, as plain as the fish in front of him, sat his beloved grandparents whom he loved, and missed, and grieved since the day they left.

The shockwave of what he saw knocked him down on all fours, dropping the fish, and stealing his breath. With his head down, he angrily cajoled himself to regain his composure, "GODDAMM IT, JACK, GET AHOLD OF YOURSELF... YOU'RE SEEING THINGS!" Jack tried to re-assure himself that what he just saw could not, *was not*, possible or real.

Seconds seemed like an eternity. The fish flopped and hit Jack's arm, and he looked at it apologetically because he had forgotten about putting him back in the water. He grabbed the fish and slid him off the dock back into the coffee-colored waters. Getting to his feet, he watched the tail disappear as he turned his head back to the bench.

They were still there, still smiling at him in the evening sun. Jack's grandfather raised his left thumb in approval over his grandson's catch while his grandmother clearly mouthed the words, "Go find him."

Jack froze, staring at them as they twinkled like they were covered with a fine dust of diamonds. He could feel the tears rolling down his cheeks and falling off his jaw as the reality of what he was seeing started to truly sink in, and the deeper it sank, the greater the fear that welled up inside of him was.

Jack blinked and wiped his eyes, and they were gone, like an executioner turning his head for a split second allowing the prisoner to escape. Jack did not hesitate for even a moment. He sprinted to the truck as an icy chill ran through his bones, leaving the tackle box on the bench and screaming out with an urgency, "FINNNNN!!!"

CHAPTER ONE

Jack had been on the road for the better part of a week, traveling west through Chicago and into Wisconsin before he stopped for the first time. Dairy farms with their lush, rolling green pastures that look like carpeting spread across the horizon, dotted with groups of brown and black cows, passing their days together as if in slow motion reminded Jack of home.

Old growth forests lined the highways and provided an impenetrable screen of leaves and branches. It seemed like a happy place through the windshield of Jack's truck, a piece of what "Americana" would look like. The hustle and bustle of the east coast and the windy city now thankfully behind him.

It had taken crossing half the country for Jack to start to settle down after what had happened back on the bank of the river. His mind had finally started to loosen its stranglehold caused by fear surrounding those events and images. He was able to take deep breaths again, while trying to put aside the image of his dead grandparents smiling and talking to him.

As Jack traveled across the Great Plains, miles per hour passed like water through his clenched fist, seeping through the cracks without him even noticing as he considered how far he had come in his life.

For Jack, those early days in the Army were the easiest of his adult life. He was removed from his family, friends, and all that he had known. The Army told him exactly where to be and when to be there, and what the expectations were once you were there. Once Jack knew what was expected of him, he had no problem fulfilling that expectation. It was all so simple.

He had always put himself in a secondary role of importance to everyone else, a habit that was very difficult to break. The stigma of doing for himself, caring for and loving himself, seemed egotistical, selfish, and self-centered.

Weary from isolation and the road, Jack crossed the Mississippi River, leaving Wisconsin in the rearview and pulled into a campsite in Minnesota to rest for the night. Through the trees, he could partially see the big river and the bluffs that made up the far shoreline, high and wide, like the padded shoulders of a giant linebacker standing guard over the undulating liquid line of scrimmage below. The sight was immediately comforting, like a security guard watching over all that passed by on its currents. This, as the young man at the check in gate had explained, was bluff country.

Jack was at once struck by the size and grandeur of the river, by the never-ending currents that flowed south to the Gulf of Mexico. As a boy, Jack had read *The Adventures of Tom Sawyer and Huckleberry Finn* countless times, absorbing every detail, imagining it in his head like a movie. He had daydreamed about riding the Mississippi River currents to far off adventures, and he had even named his dog Fin in their honor. He had also named him after the fins on a fish. Fishing is life for Jack, and Fin is his closest friend. As a puppy, he had always tried to take a bite out of every fish Jack caught, so the name Fin stuck.

The young man at the check-in gate had been informative and enthusiastic and given him some great information in a very short amount of time, even suggested a hike with amazing views of the river. Jack was glad he had stayed out of his own head long enough to listen to his suggestions because they had been cooped up long enough in the truck and desperately needed some fresh air and to stretch their legs.

The trail was three miles to the overlook, the last mile uphill. Covered in sweat and both panting when they arrived, Jack stood catching his breath and looking at the river when an object caught his eye. A boat was in the river, slowly moving north against the massive current making very slow headway, like it was laboring against the heavy flow.

Jack had spent his life on the water, in lakes and rivers, learning the ways of the waves and currents and how they react, but this stuck out to him for some reason.

This was the first time that he could remember looking at current as a combined force or energy as it went on its way down river. It was the boat versus the current and the boat had to continue going forward against the current.

As the boat in the distance stood mired in place, Jack thought about its options. Backward was known, same old shit, always dealt with it and he supposed in the face of an uncertain future he could deal with it again, at least it was known. Forward held opportunity for a different outcome, a potentially better one, but also a possibly worse one, and it was completely unknown.

Jack was still looking at the boat making its way against the current when he realized what it meant. Grief had mired him for twenty years since the death of his grandparents and kept him in mid-current, just like the boat he was watching, and he had no flaming idea how to stop doing it. And now, heaped on top of that was what had transpired back along the river on base, what it meant and how to handle it.

Standing there on that bluff, in the blazing sun of a summer afternoon, overlooking a landscape that he had never seen before, the tears streamed uncontrollably down his face over the two people he had lost, a life he'd been too terrified to live, and the journey to find a man who didn't exist. Overwhelmed, the soldier wept silently.

"Don't be a deterrent to the current."

The man's voice crackled dangerously close behind Jack's right ear as it pierced the natural silence around him. He spun with lightning quickness as his fists instinctively clenched in anticipation of a close quarters assault. Cocking his right arm, his eyes met the eyes behind the voice.

"WHOA, WHOA, WHOA!" the man yelled, as he backpedaled away from Jack with both hands raised in surrender. "I mean you no harm boy. I didn't realize I would startle you like this."

"Where the FUCK did you come from?" hissed off Jack's tongue like a snake that just had its tail stepped on. "How did you sneak up on me, *and* my dog unnoticed?"

"I was just out for an afternoon hike, like you."

"Bullshit! You're not even sweating, or the least bit out of breath after coming up that hill."

The first punch was still cocked in his right arm and ready to be thrown. His military training had taken over and he was assessing the threat level of someone who had appeared out of nowhere. The man's story was illogical, so it must be false and hiding an ulterior motive.

"I really didn't mean to frighten you on our first meeting. I thought you were ready. Maybe I should go."

Fin caught Jack's attention. He stood wagging his tail at the man. It struck him as odd that the dog looked like he wanted to play, when Jack felt like he wanted to kill. This guy had caught Jack so off guard that it rocked him harder than he was prepared to handle. He looked back at the man to try and deescalate the situation, but he was gone.

"Where the hell did he go, boy?" The adrenaline returned so strongly that he could feel his still clenched fists shaking. "How the hell did he breach our perimeter undetected and then disappear just as quickly?"

Dog and Man walked to the edge and looked over where the trail descended down the sparsely vegetated slope of the bluff. Jack could see all the way to the bottom where the trail wound off into the woods over a mile away, but there was no sign of the man anywhere in sight. Dumbfounded by the events of the last few minutes, Jack continued to stare down the slope trying to piece together everything that had happened.

"C'mon Fin. It's time to head back." When they reached the bottom of the hill, they passed a small group of hikers on their way up.

"Hey, cool dog," said one of the young hikers as he stooped to pet Fin.

"You see a guy pass by?" Jack asked them.

"Sorry, dude, no" said the hiker.

Jack smiled and bid them good day and continued on so as not to raise any further questions that he was unable to answer.

The memories that had come to the surface during the hike were powerful, and when given attention, elicited the same response from Jack that they always had…pain, guilt, and fear.

Loneliness and isolation were feelings that Jack knew all too well. He also knew that if left unchecked inside of him, they would render him catatonic. So, he spun it and spun it in an attempt to comfort himself, to avoid thinking about the revelations of the last ten days, or the last hour.

CHAPTER TWO

It was late in the day as Jack drove west into South Dakota, the sun was getting low on the horizon and into his eyes. Today's drive for Jack had consisted of mentally replaying what had happened on the trail yesterday, going over every action and reaction trying to figure out how a man got inside his kill circle undetected and then vanish into thin air just as quickly.

He realized during the days' worth of replays that he had never felt like he was in danger from the man, even after having been startled so severely, and he mused, "If I weren't in such a deep state of self-pity, I might have heard him coming."

A flat, empty horizon marked by billboards for Wall Drugs every mile along the Interstate cajoled drivers to stop and have a five-cent cup of coffee. Succumbing to the barrage of advertising as the exit sign said one mile, he stopped to see what the signs were all about.

Jack wanted to dismiss the whole incident as random, and he tried to do just that for hundreds of miles leading up to pulling into the parking lot of the five-cent coffee capitol of the world, but it didn't make sense to him, so it wouldn't go away.

Jack wandered aimlessly around the many buildings of Wall Drug for over an hour without seeing anything that interested him enough to stop. He soon realized that he had left Fin cooped up in the truck long enough, and it was time to find a place to settle in for the night.

The time spent in the store was filled with images and thoughts about the last two weeks of his life. Seeing his deceased grandparents breathing and smiling at him, the curious boat fighting against the unyielding current of the Mississippi River, and the pierced tranquility of his hike by a man he could not get out of his head.

How had he appeared and disappeared without a trace? Jack always felt a sense of emptiness, always missing pieces of his life's puzzle, but today it felt like he was missing a piece of his mind and sanity. His veiled attempt at taking his mind off of things by staring at trinkets had come to an end and Jack headed back out to the truck with coffee in hand and ninety-five cents that jingled in his pocket.

The parking lot was just as jammed as he exited the building as it had been when he arrived, and the truck was parked half a football field away, but the distance and the bustle could not mask a familiar sound in Jack's ears. The sound was Fin barking in the truck.

The first thought in Jack's head was that kids were teasing him through the window and he was telling them to either buzz off, or to open the door so he could play with them, but the closer he got to where the truck was parked the more intense the barking became. Something was clearly wrong, Jack broke into a sprint, dropping his coffee along the way.

Arriving at the truck, he instantly saw what was causing the commotion. The cap door on the truck bed was wide open and one of the two rod cases containing his favorite fly rod was gone. His whole body went numb; his head had been filled with so much shit when he had pulled in, he had forgotten to lock the back of the truck.

"How could you be so fucking stupid, you worthless piece of shit!" The self-attack was swift, merciless, and unrelenting. Each tirade of profanity, anger, and shame cut deeper than the previous one. "Unfucking-believable! We're on a cross country fishing trip, and now I don't have my favorite goddamn ROD, all because you let some old guy sneak up and spook the shit out of you like he was Casper the friendly fucking ghost!"

Jack stood with his head down resting his weight on the tail-gate of the truck as his internal voice destroyed him over his negligence. He wanted to cry, to kill, to run away, and to pretend like it had never happened, but he was already doing that. So, he did what he always did, he swallowed all of it and locked it inside.

Sitting in the huge parking lot now behind the drug store he stared blankly into space, he had no one to blame but himself. There were no rods to set up for the next day on the Bighorn River and no excitement building in his belly.

Gone were the visions of rising trout, and fishing trips with Gramp of years past. Those had been special days, meaningful days, traditions they had shared that were the fibers of an unbreakable bond with a man who was everything to him.

Now, he would arrive tomorrow in Fort Smith, Montana, under a grey cloud instead of on the promise of a new day.

CHAPTER THREE

Jack's internal alarm clock was always set, even when he did not want it to be. Tardiness is the ultimate failure in his mind. His Gramp had a simple rule for Jack, if he was not up and ready to go, then he was left home.

Today Jack awoke, alone, and locked inside the cap of the truck. There was no one to please, and no one to be excited with. Jack had felt a sense of emptiness all his life, always missing the imaginary father he hadn't known.

Jack's fear of rejection and intimacy was a direct result of never being able to finish his own puzzle because of the missing piece that represented his father. Until the day on the dock, he could never explain how it left him feeling incomplete. He only had half a story and didn't know how to handle it.

As close as he was to his grandparents, he never once talked about it because he feared it would seem as though he was ungrateful, or worse, that he would make them feel as though they weren't enough for him. Jack could not bear the thought of hurting their feelings, so he didn't, but the feelings never went away.

The image of the small boat battling the currents of the mighty Mississippi River flashed into Jack's mind. The current is the natural way of the river - its purpose is to flow downstream.

"The man yesterday on the trail said something about the current before things went haywire... what the hell was it he said?"

Fin heard Jack talking and opened his eyes to see what was going on and if he should get up for it. So as Jack made himself coffee on the tailgate of the truck, Fin decided to hop down out of bed, stretch his long, sleek, black body, sneeze repeatedly, shake his face as if to wake himself up, and proceed to the nearest truck tire to relieve himself.

"You have quite the personality, mutt. I have never known another dog who sneezes or puts on quite the show that you do." Fin returned, unaware of the amusement he had provided, and came to Jack's side and sat.

Begrudgingly, Jack got down on one knee and rubbed his face and ears. Fin's eyes never blinked, or left Jack's face as he wrapped his arms around the old dog's neck and squeezed him. Jack was in desperate need of a little kindness, and thankfully his faithful companion was always willing to oblige him, and then his memory popped like corn.

"I remember! He said don't be a deterrent to the current." the words rang out, "Don't be a deterrent to the current!" is that what he said? His body immediately vibrated internally like it had done on base that night.

The words he had just spoken elicited the same response as the day on the dock when he was directed to go and find his father. Instinctively he knew he was on to something as he continued to talk through the thoughts that were exploding in his head like firecrackers.

"The boat was acting as a deterrent to the current, impeding its progress, and the river's natural way of being. That must be why it stuck out to me so much. I am a deterrent to my own current, my own flow."

The theories strung together in Jack's mind, clear and precise and he instantly accepted them without hesitation.

"My grief has held me in midstream for so many years. I wonder if that's why my grandparents told me to go and try to find my father, so I would get out of my own way and let the current move me along in life?"

Jack made eye contact with Fin as he finished asking the question;

this foreign vibration tickling up his spine had started to become familiar now and only seemed to occur in response to a direct question. Some things were making sense to him, but the questions of who the man was, why he said that phrase, and how he appeared and disappeared - seemingly into thin air - were still unanswered.

CHAPTER FOUR

The exit sign for Lodge Grass whizzed by the passenger side window of the truck and reminded him that in one mile he would need to exit the highway and head west up over the mountains to the Big Horn River valley. Jack adjusted in the driver's seat, pulling himself forward over the steering wheel to stretch his back, but the reality of the maneuver was to clear his mind, to get away from the string of thoughts and the reactions he kept experiencing.

Frightened was not what Jack was feeling. He knew in the deepest recesses of his being there was far more to this life than met the eye, but, in this moment, like every other moment in his life to date, he passed his thoughts and feelings off as coincidental, frivolous, or more accurately, as unworthy.

Being unworthy was a recurring theme for him. Who was he anyway to think he might be special? He was Jackson Straw, a bastard child, who had been abandoned by his own father. Who was he to have insight into anything, let alone anything potentially supernatural? His anger welled up as he dismissed himself once again.

"Just keep driving, Jack; live in the real-world, Jack; stop with these thoughts. We're nobody; we're not going to figure out or discover some universal truth that people much smarter than we have not been able to figure out, so just leave it alone, and get on with your life in the tangible world that we can see and feel and stop worrying about what is beyond our sight."

Jack stopped thinking. The voice in his head was so cruel, so derogatory and degrading. No one had ever spoken to him in life like he spoke to himself in his head. His head hung low, like a beaten dog as he came to a stop at the bottom of the off-ramp.

He was surrounded by spectacular scenery - glorious and grand on a scale that was unimaginable. It made Jack feel very small in comparison. He gave a resilient nod to his belief in the universe being much bigger than our little part in it.

Cresting the west slope, Jack saw the river below and the beauty diverted his attention away from his masochistic self-talk. If this destination was a pilgrimage for him, then he was pulling into the parking lot of his High Temple as the sign above the door read "Big Horn Trout Shop."

Normally for Jack, a foray into a place like this was merely to window shop, to look around at the offerings, possibly buy a token of his trip or to add to his collection of t-shirts. But, today he is a consumer. Some son-of-a-bitch had seen to that when he had stolen his rods out of the back of the truck. Even if it were unlocked, Jack thought to himself, what kind of man steals another man's fishing rod?

Soon he was back in the truck with the new rod stowed in the back, pissed and stewing at the whole situation that had forced him to spend a fair chunk of money on something that twenty-four hours ago he hadn't needed or wanted.

"Let's go fishing, boy, and forget about this whole thing."

He could hear the rumbling murmur of the river as it greeted him when he arrived. Water makes a variety of sounds as it moves over the rocky bottom of the river. Today, it sounded like a conversation between old friends, happy, inviting, and bubbly. Jack knew to appreciate his time on the water, and the warm greeting from the river washed away everything else.

His heart beat wildly; hands sweaty, new rod in hand, he walked toward a childhood dream. In his brain, Jack tried to figure out how he was going to take a picture of himself and his first Big Horn Trout.

Jack caught movement off to his right in the far end of the parking lot - a man getting out of his car and walking around to open the tailgate. No acknowledgement for Jack, just a passing visual that had caught his attention. His pace quickened, eyes now locked over the bank scanning the currents. Forgotten now was the fear that had sent him running two thousand miles and the strange circumstances that had surrounded him on this trip.

Stripping line off the reel he started his false casts until he had enough line suspended in the air over his head to reach the feeding fish. Before he can let the cast go, the loop crumbled behind him, and the ensuing forward stroke resulted in a mass of line and leader falling into the water at his feet with a heavy splash.

"What the fuck!" Jack snapped, his eyes still fixated on the dimples scattered across the slick current caused by the feeding trout. He untangled the line quickly and started the process again, and again the same result. This new rod had a much different action than the rod he was familiar with, but there was no time to practice or slowly figure it out. He was in trout Mecca of the world with actively feeding fish right in front of him and he couldn't even cast.

"Why the fuck did I buy this new rod?" Jack said bitterly, "because I was so stupid as to not lock the truck, that's why. I can't even cast this fucking thing."

That horrible beratement of himself opened the flood gates to anger, doubt, and self-loathing. The tidal wave washed Jack away in an instant and the rest of his afternoon of fishing was filled with frustrating casts, poor execution, missed strikes, and failure. Each incident was like pouring gasoline on the raging fire burning inside of him.

His expectations were so high, so built up for what was supposed to be the best fishing day of his life, that he only focused on what was not going according to his elaborate plan, and it was completely ruining his experience. He himself could not live up to the pressure he applied, nor could the fishing. He had successfully set himself up for failure.

By the time the sun was dipping behind the mountains to the west Jack was sitting on the gravel bar, head slumped down into his hands, eyes glazed, unmoving. Fin had seen this behavior before from Jack and knew enough to keep his distance when Jack was like this, so he lay curled in a ball a few feet away, silent and unmoving, so as to not incur Jack's wrath.

The brilliant orange of the sunset that was highlighted with streaks of purple and pink lit Jack's face, but he never looked up. His mind frozen in failure.

Finally, he stood up and grabbed his gear, beaten and exhausted from the rage that had consumed him all afternoon.

"Let's go, boy, before it's pitch dark."

The parking lot was vacant when Jack and Fin returned to the truck well past dark. The walk back had not quelled any of the negative thoughts or voices inside of Jack, in fact they were getting louder. Jack's ego was screaming in his ear with every step he took, "You failed, let's get the fuck out of here, you aren't good enough to be successful on this river." The repetition of negativity circled like a whirlpool inside of Jack.

Unlocking the truck, he hung the little battery-operated lantern from the cap, fed Fin, and sat down. He took a long sip of the beer he had retrieved from the cooler and exhaled mightily as if to try and let everything roll off him. The theory was sound, but in practice, it did not work.

He sat in the little circle of light its beam engulfing him with the infinity of darkness outside. The sky was clear and moonless as he gazed at the millions of tiny lights that dotted the western sky. He was here, on the banks of the Big Horn River, a place he had always dreamed of being, a place and time that he had looked forward to for as long as he could remember. How, he pondered, had everything gone so terribly wrong?

"Am I just not good enough to be successful here on this river, or in life for that matter?" No anger emanated from inside when he said those words, Jack simply accepted them as the truth, his truth, as he stared at the blanket of stars undulating above his head and covering him up for the night.

CHAPTER FIVE

He woke to the same darkness he had left a couple of hours earlier, only the blanket of stars was much thinner now. When Jack sat up, Fin stirred for the first time. He had gotten up in the truck and lain on his comfy bed to keep watch over Jack, who had slept all night in the chair with his beer can still firm in his grip.

Jack pulled out the little camp stove as he wiped sleep from his eyes, lit and covered the flame with a percolator full of water and coffee grounds. In fifteen minutes, the world would calm down and Jack would be able to think everything through as he sipped his first cup.

Jack noticed the headlamps bobbing and weaving on the other side of the lot where three groups of Anglers were getting ready for a day's fishing with their guides. He thought about how much agony could have been avoided if he would have just hired a guide to show and tell him everything he needed to know instead of insisting on doing it himself.

"Obviously, I am not able to be successful on my own," he whispered to himself. He did not trust his own instincts or abilities, and the negativity manifested exactly what he truly believed.

This silent conversation was shattered like a plate glass mirror as a voice cleared his throat behind him, "Excuse me."

Startled, Fin snapped his head around but never made a peep, and immediately went to the outstretched hand, attached to the arm, that belonged to the voice for a pet from a stranger in the dark. Following suit, Jack spun around so fast he almost threw himself off balance.

He searched in the darkness to find the face behind the voice. Under the light above the tailgate he saw the face he had watched get out of the car yesterday when he had arrived in the parking lot. It did not look familiar, only that he vaguely recognized it.

A smile crossed the face that Jack was looking at. In the dim light, his lips that were surrounded by a silver goatee parted slowly, "I'm so sorry, boy. I didn't mean to startle you again."

Jack looked at his eyes, quickly, directly, for any signs of what his intentions might be. He could not pick up anything, but every muscle was tense, fists clenched at his side ready to attack or defend, but no reaction came.

"My name is Stu." The man raised his hand from petting Fin and stretched it toward Jack in a gentlemanly greeting. "I smelled your coffee from my vehicle on the other side of the lot and thought I would come over and say good morning and see if you might offer me a cup before we head to the river?"

"We?" Jack murmured.

"Yes, I'm the guide you just asked for," Stu said with a wry smile. "And don't be so hard on the dog. He's a good boy, a good judge of character. He knew I meant you no harm."

Jack stood motionless for a moment looking at the outstretched hand. Where did this guy come from? He did not remember seeing another vehicle in the lot when he had returned to the truck last night and there had only been the three guide trucks that pulled into the lot this morning.

He was not himself yesterday, or lately for that matter he thought. Maybe he was not paying attention and missed it, but he never missed anything, so, how in the hell did this guy sneak into his perimeter undetected by him *and* the dog? That's just not possible. It was like he had just appeared out of nowhere. The thought came to his mind that this had happened twice now in the last three days.

Jack felt a tingling sensation with that realization, not a danger alert, more like a déjà vu. It tickled through him from head to toe as his questions remained, but his resistance was fading away quickly, melting into the unexplainable feeling of a normal meeting with an old friend.

Jack shook Stu's outstretched hand. "Please excuse my behavior. Stu, is it? You gave me quite a start. I'm not accustomed to being surprised by anything, or anyone. My name is Jack and that mush of a guard dog you are petting is…"

"Fin," Stu interjected. "I know, I heard you calling his name yesterday."

"You heard me?" Jack fired back. "When? Where?"

"Down on the river," Stu said. "You were out on the gravel bar. At first, I thought you were having a great day, then it became clear you were not. Your yells and screams were out of frustration, not jubilance, so I stayed clear of you instead of wandering over to say hello and share stories of the day. Last I saw, you were sitting with your head down, missing the most beautiful sunset imaginable."

Jack stiffened "I did not see you or anyone else all afternoon yesterday! Where were you, that you saw me?"

Stu looked at Jack kindly, as if to reassure him that this revelation, like startling him just now, was ok. "You were on the river first, you saw me in the parking lot as you walked by. I passed behind you and went down river of you, and then made my way back to the parking lot as the last rays of light lit up the river. The fish were rising up like birds right in front of you as the day ended."

Jack shook his head. "That's not possible. You're saying that you passed behind me twice yesterday and I never saw you either time?"

"Yes, that's exactly what I'm saying," Stu replied. "From the looks of it, you couldn't see anything beyond your anger."

"I don't know what to say, Stu. I have been trained all my life to be alert and vigilant. Now in the span of 24 hours, you have skirted my flank twice and made it into my camp, scaring the shit out of me, and to rub salt in an open wound, I failed so miserably yesterday doing the one thing that I truly love, suddenly nothing seems to make any sense."

"Well, boy, I was trained as well, to be a ghost in a distant jungle, to be undetectable, to do things that cannot be undone, and I was very good at it. There is no failure, only learning. Remember that."

Jack stood like a statue frozen in time as chills ran through his body staring at this man in the dark. The only person in the world to ever call him "boy" was his grandfather, and he said it in the same loving, calming way Stu had just done. Jack didn't know how his mind worked, but it was suddenly crystal clear. This man had called him boy moments ago as well as the man on the trail back in Minnesota, but before he could connect the dots, Stu interjected.

"Stop being so hard on yourself all the time. Show yourself a little love and kindness once in a while. You extend kindness and patience to everyone but yourself."

Who are you? What are you? Why are you here with me? Questions rolled around in Jack's head, but he couldn't get his lips to say the words aloud. Given the circumstances, maybe he didn't really want to know the answers.

"Can we have that coffee now?" Stu asked. "It's done, and the sun is coming up. We definitely want to be on the river when the morning hatch starts."

Jack poured with shaking hands. "What do you mean WE want to be on the river by sunrise? I'm not fishing today."

"You asked for a guide, and here I am, at your service, sir."

"I heard you say you were a guide earlier, but I just assumed you were a trout bum looking for a free cup of coffee, someone to talk to, and a tip at the end of the day, not an actual, licensed, fishing guide like I asked for under my breath five seconds before you appeared."

Sarcasm and a tinge of exasperation colored Jack's statement, but Stu continued unaffected.

"Well, what else would I be doing out here on the river? Spirit guiding? Life coaching? Of course not, even though fishing *is* spirit and life mixed together. I'm just an old river rat looking to share a day of liquid meditation with someone who could use my assistance."

"I'm sorry to disappoint you then, because I'm getting on the road as soon as this coffee is done, and the truck is packed. I had enough yesterday to last me a good long while. Besides, I have to make a stop in town before I get on the road which is the only reason why I haven't left yet and why you even had the opportunity to sneak up on me."

"You're going to return that beautiful new rod before you go?"

"Yes… wait. How do you know about the rod?"

Stu smiled and pointed to it glistening against the lightening eastern sky. "It's right there, it looks brand new, I admired it in your hand yesterday when the rod wrappings caught the sunlight. I thought it looked like a woman's manicured fingernails."

Jack did not reply, but he had thought the same thing about the rod and the wrappings when he had first seen it, and now Stu said the exact thing he had thought. A chill of recognition ran up his spine combined with him calling him "boy" and the déjà vu feeling of knowing him from somewhere.

"Yes, if you must know, I'm returning the rod to the fly shop. I didn't really care for it after all."

Laughing out loud, Stu looked Jack in the eyes. "And it didn't work worth a shit either, did it? Before Jack could answer the sarcastic rhetorical question, Stu tugged him by the arm, "Come on boy, let's go fishing, just for a couple of hours. You can rush out of here and be on your way to wherever you are heading after that. You're ready this time and I would enjoy the company and conversation, so humor an old man, will ya?"

Jack looked down at Stu, who was sitting in the chair that Jack had slept in last night. Even though Jack assumed Stu had been in Vietnam, and that made him at least seventy-ish years old, Stu did not look or act that old. He obviously still moved like a cat, and his face, framed with grey hair and chin whiskers, still had a youthful look to it. Jack thought to himself that if he looked that good at Stu's age then he would he pretty happy.

"Humor an old man, huh?" retorted Jack as he surprised himself by smiling back at Stu. "Then move your ass, old man, or I'm going without you."

Stu got up and hunched over, moving the chair from side to side in his hand like an old man with a cane that was too wobbly to stand, and grabbed his lower back in a sarcastic gesture while mumbling under his breath, "I'm glad to see you actually have a sense of humor underneath all that scowl, just like he said you did."

"What the hell did you say?"

Clearing his throat dramatically with the wry smile returning to his face he looked at Jack, "I didn't say anything. Now get your gear on, boy, or I'll leave *you*!" Stu turned and walked away.

Jack hurriedly dressed and caught up with him on the far side of the parking lot. Against all his protests, his excitement built with each step. As they walked with the rising sun behind them toward the river, Jack stopped on the trail in mid-step. The light caught his eye as he looked to the west to see the mountains illuminated by the rising sun like someone was shining a spotlight on them. It was the first time in days when he had stopped to soak in where he was and what he was seeing, and it was magnificent, a breathtaking sight to behold.

Jack stood there in the moment and soaked it all in, his surroundings, the scenery, the feeling of renewal a sunrise brings, the beginning of a fresh new day. He forgot about casting or catching in that moment - he thought only about what his eyes were witnessing.

"Pretty amazing, isn't it?" Stu asked.

"Damn you, old man, quit sneaking up on me, and scaring the shit out of me like that, please!"

"Then pay attention for once, and maybe you won't be so scared of everything that pops up in front of your eyes, and I'll show you who's an old man when I out-fish you today," Stu said shaking his fist in the air over his head, smiling and muttering.

CHAPTER SIX

Taking a deep breath, he unhooked the fly from the rod in preparation of his first cast. He couldn't shake the feeling that he was returning to the scene of a grizzly crime. "*If today is going to be a repeat of yesterday,*" Jack whispered to himself, "*I don't know if I can handle it.*"

Stu was just down river readying for his first cast when he looked at Jack and then pointed with his rod tip to the far bank where, almost undetectably, there were trout sipping insects off the surface.

After a second or two of studying the surface Jack saw what Stu was pointing at; both men made eye contact and smiled like a cat that was about to pounce on the canary.

"Pay close attention to what you are doing today, trust your instincts, and don't be a deterrent to the current."

What did he mean by that? I don't understand, and how the hell does he know, or think he knows I was not paying attention yesterday? He only walked by me from a distance, he could not have possibly ascertained all of this information just from passing by, Jack thought.

Then, Jack turned to stone as Stu's words penetrated his ears and seeped into his conscious brain. The symphony of thoughts, emotions, and voices in his head played to a frenzied crescendo, and then silenced as the blurry picture came into high definition focus in his mind's eye.

That is the phrase the man on the trail in Minnesota said when he appeared out of nowhere. That isn't a common phrase, nor have I ever heard it used before, this can't be a coincidence. These were the thoughts running through Jack's mind like a herd of buffalo rumbling across the prairie.

Then the picture came into focus just as the words did and Jack could see the smile, that, "I know something that you don't know yet," wry smile that was on the man's face from the trail and on *STU'S* face. "HOLY SHIT, STU IS THE MAN FROM MINNESOTA!" And, with that statement the thunder crashed down on Jack's head and vibrated him to his core.

Jack was stalling, the questions and thoughts in his head were running roughshod, but he was just standing there, not fishing. His deepest thoughts and most in-depth conversations of his life had come to him while fishing. It was an unconscious act for him, and yet here he stood like a statue no longer afraid to cast his line out of fear of failure.

Jack's eyes found Stu, who looked to be in his own world, as he watched him from a distance, lit up in the morning sun like his body was surrounded by a glowing golden halo. Jack noticed how the droplets of water looked like they were suspended in time as his fly line snaked effortlessly through the morning air with each cast.

"Pay attention," Stu's voice whispered in his ears.

Jack snapped around to look for Stu. Even though he was looking right at him, the whisper sounded like it was directly behind him. Jack checked in both directions, then looked back at Stu twenty feet away, oblivious to Jack's stare. Jack bent down and untangled his line once again, talking to himself to ward off the feelings of losing his mind. "This absurd trip is fucking with me," his voice hushed so only he could hear, "why am I here?"

"Ready for a break yet?" Stu asked, suddenly standing right in front of him, and shattering Jack's internal monologue. "By the looks of your casting, I assume you are."

"For Christ sakes, Stu," Jack's whole body convulsed from the shock of being startled, again, "will you please stop doing that to me? And you can kiss my ass about my casting. It's the rod, it's clearly defective, which is why I said I was returning it this morning."

Stu chuckled heartily at Jack's reasoning, "Sorry boy, I just thought you might want to join me on the log for a little break. I'm really not trying to give you a heart attack. I'll try to announce myself in advance from now on so that you are aware of me coming toward you. I promise."

The tight, tanned skin, the dark sunglasses contrasting with the silvery white hair and the matching color stubble on his chin could not hide the mischievous grin plastered across his face as he pledged to Jack not to scare him anymore.

"It's not funny old man, you're like a *ghost,* levitating all around the river and sneaking up on me all the time like we're back in the jungle."

He had not asked Stu what he did in the Army - he would never ask - but it was blatantly obvious that Stu was not some supply sergeant. He had been in the thick of battles and the scars he carried with him were unseen by outside eyes, but still very much there.

The corners of Stu's mouth stretched upward, exposing his teeth and creating a wide and kind smile. "Well then maybe you don't need a break. What do I know? I'm just a ghost after all."

Jack stood there, speechless, as Stu took the rod from his hand, "Let me try this beauty, I mean defective piece of crap, out for myself." In three false casts, Stu had stripped out fifty feet of line and suspended it in midair over his head like a snake charmer coercing the cobra out of a basket. The fly landed and had scarcely traveled two feet in the rumbling, bubbling current when it disappeared from sight after the trout had eaten it.

Stu put the rod back in Jack's hand after releasing the fish he had just landed and walked over to the weathered, bark-stripped log that the current had placed in the center of the gravel bar and sat down. Jack was smiling ear to ear at what he had just witnessed as he looked up at Stu sitting on the log.

Stu smiled back. "I'm not sure what the problem is. That new rod seems to work just fine to me!"

Jack was amazed that the rod had worked - befuddled might be more accurate - of course Jack knew the rod worked, his claim of defect was a ruse. It is a fly rod, a very expensive, high-end, artfully crafted fly rod, designed to cast a fly line better than can be imagined. It worked just fine. It was Jack that was not working.

"Are you ready to get out of your own way?"

"Your timing is impeccable as always, but I don't know how to answer your question."

"For the last two days you've been out of sorts, uncomfortable in your own skin."

"It's been longer than that."

"You're angry that you are here alone, without your grandfather to share this with. That anger has energy that has to go somewhere so you aimed it at yourself and now it's standing in the way of what you love the most. What you're not realizing is that your Gramp has been sitting right next to you since you arrived here."

Jack snapped his head upward to meet Stu's gaze, "You mean metaphorically, right?"

"No, I mean literally, he has not been more than a foot away from you since you arrived."

"My Gramp is not here, and even if he were, neither you nor I could, or would, be able to see him. He has been gone for fifteen years now."

"That's not true because you have seen him, haven't you?"

Frozen, Jack stared at Stu as he spoke.

"You got exactly what you have always asked, prayed and begged for. You got to see them again, but you were not prepared for your own reaction."

"I…I... I"

"Do you really think he would miss this epic fishing trip over something as trivial as death? For that matter, do you really think either of them would let their love for you die just because their physical bodies did?"

"What are you're trying to sell me on?"

"You know this is not a coincidence that we met this morning and you already know that we have met before."

Jack absorbed these revelations with his mouth agape as he hung on Stu's every word.

"You are 2,500 miles from home, and you don't even know why. You are purposely deterring yourself from learning and seeing the truth, and you shun all that is in your best and highest good."

"Tell me what to do, tell me the answers to the millions of questions that I have then."

"I'm not here to give you answers. You already have the answers. Now is your chance to walk away if that is what you choose, or you can sit, and talk with me."

CHAPTER SEVEN

Sitting on the log next to Stu in the warm summer sun felt very comfortable. There was no pause in conversation or awkwardness between them. Spending time with this man that he had only met that morning felt easy, natural, and familiar.

Jack sat in contemplative silence with the question Stu had just asked him. Did he want to sit and talk to him? To listen and learn whatever he was about to share? What if he has answers to the questions, I have asked my whole life? What can one man share with another man that is truly insightful? What does he know, that I, or anyone else, does not already know? The questions seemed endless until a little light went off inside of him; he was going to get right to the heart of the matter.

"Who the fuck are you, Stu!" The tone and tenor of Jack's voice was sharp, much harsher than he had intended, and he knew it as soon as the words passed over his lips.

Stu held out his hand as if to say that it was all right, but Jack interjected again.

"NO! It is not all right. I let my emotions and frustrations get the better of me, just like I have been for the last two days, well, two weeks actually. I truly don't understand why or how I am even here in the first place. Less than two weeks ago I was a soldier awaiting retirement, now I am sitting here talking to you like we have known each other all our lives when, in reality, I only met you this morning. I do not like myself when I get like this. I lose control, and then my wheels start to spin like they are on a patch of ice."

"Do you want to know your grandfather's best trait?" Stu interjected into Jack's monologue. "It was that he liked himself! In fact, he loved himself, which allowed him to love everyone else in his life." Stu patted Jack on the shoulder reassuringly as he spoke. "He understood early in his life that in order to give love to others, he had to be able to be loving to himself first."

Jack started to respond to what Stu had just said but was cut off.

"Listen to my words Jack, really hear what I am telling you. Do not listen with the sole intent to respond or focus on certain words only to formulate a response. Pay full attention. Listen with the intent to feel and completely hear and understand the whole message you are hearing. Stories are just stories and the who, what, and when are interchangeable. The meanings are the lessons that are intended to help you find your own answers, to draw your own conclusions," stated Stu.

"So what lesson am I learning by being here? Why did I run away when I saw the two people I love the most? Why did they tell me to go and find a father that never knew or cared about me? Answer me those questions!"

"I can't give you answers, and even if I did, without learning the lessons on your own, the answers you got would be meaningless. Reward without effort is empty. It holds no value because you didn't earn it."

"Teachers are supposed to give you answers Stu, that's how it works. You get the answer to the problem, you study the answer, and then you put the correct answer on the test."

"That is completely wrong. The boat stuck with you when you saw it in the river that day for a reason. Even before I arrived you were fixated on it. You realized it was purposely holding itself back by trying to fight against the massive current. The boat was acting as a deterrent to the natural flow of the current, and for the first time in your life you recognized it as being synonymous with yourself, not knowing yet what it really meant."

"So, I am the boat?" Jack asked. "I am the deterrent to my own current, and the current represents my life?"

"It's not just your life Jack. The current represents the true meaning of why you are here on this earth, in this time, in this body. Your soul purposely chose this life to learn a very specific lesson. The current is a life that is fulfilling to you on a deeper level, not superficially, or coincidentally. Once we learn the lesson we came here for we graduate to the next life. In soul terms, we ascend."

"So, I am here for a reason, at this very moment, sitting on this log with you, learning a single lesson that is fundamental to my personal and spiritual growth? Is that what you are saying?" Jack asked.

"No Jack, that is what you're saying," Stu said as he smiled at him. "You and I being here in this moment is necessary to awaken you to the fact that you have a purpose. It's your mission now to go find what that purpose is. Your life will change for the better, can only change, once you identify, understand, and seek your life's true meaning."

The thoughts were crystal clear in Jack's mind, the cymbals were crashing heavy with each new revelation. He was no longer questioning who this man was, or if his message was valid. He didn't care. He could feel the authenticity, everything ringing true in Jack's ears.

"That was why you told me to pay attention, to get out of my own way, and why you just gave me the example of Gramp because I have to love myself before I could ever love another, wasn't it?"

The vibrations from the crashing cymbals inside of Jack were deafening. He had started to stand up but stayed seated as the emotions overwhelmed him. "I don't want to be a deterrent to myself any longer. I want to be the opposite. What *is* the opposite, Stu?"

"I don't know. Maybe you should look it up in a dictionary and find your own answer," he said with a sheepish grin. "Oh, one last thing

Jack. They are two of the nicest people I have ever had the pleasure of meeting."

"*Meeting*?" Jack stuttered. "You met my grandparents? Where? When? How?"

"Yes, I met them, and your grandfather just reminded me that we have been sitting here for hours and the afternoon hatch is starting right in front of us, so quit talking and grab your rod quick and let's get out there!"

Revelations of the universe were still spinning in the air like the swarms of insects coming off the Montana river in the late summer sun. Stu's statement reached Jack's brain and he looked up to see the bugs flying off the surface of the water. He could hear the sound of trout feeding, like someone slurping soup one spoonful at a time and everything else in the world faded away, even this newest twist.

Three quick steps from the log to the water's edge and Jack picked up his rod, unhooked the fly, stripped off enough line to make the cast, and suspended it in mid-air over his head like a cobra under the spell of a snake charmer. Effortlessly, instinctively, and absent of thought each false cast gained distance and speed as his wading boots struck the water's edge.

Jack disengaged from his doubt-filled subconscious mind and locked onto a target, rolled his wrist over like he had done thousands of times before and delivered a perfect strike. Instantly the fly disappeared with a gulp, and the tip snapped skyward with authority. Jack's primeval scream of joy echoed across time and space, reverberating off the mountains fifty miles away, and the crowd was instantly on their feet, cheering wildly in his head.

"*I did it! I did it! I fucking did it*!"

The profanity bellowing off Jack's lips was filled with gratitude and thanks for this moment. Jack actually thanked himself for once, with the same level of kindness and sincerity he would thank another person.

He automatically looked for Stu to share this moment, to hold up his prize for him to see just like he would do with gramp, and found him still sitting on the log, not having moved an inch, watching his every move, with a proud smile on his face. He raised his thumb high in the air as congratulations.

"*Well done, boy*! See what happens when you're no longer the deterrent?"

CHAPTER EIGHT

The rest of the afternoon was pure magic on that little gravel bar in the middle of the Big Horn River two friends sharing a summer afternoon in the shadow of the Rocky Mountains and a fishing experience beyond their wildest dreams.

"Why are you just standing there smiling and not fishing?"

"Oh, sorry", Jack replied, "I was just thinking about something."

"What?"

"Fishing is what I enjoy most in life, it's my favorite hobby and can be argued that it's no hobby at all. To *say* it is merely a hobby dismisses its importance and diminishes the value of the lessons that it teaches. I have never seen anyone unhappy while reeling in a fish, like it's some kind of therapy."

Stu nodded his head as he replied. "**Nothing is ever any one thing all the time**." To be a fisherman is to be patient, yet patience does not mean inactivity, it means to have faith in yourself and your ability. Someone can tell you exactly where to fish, when to fish and what to use, and you may be successful following their directions, but that doesn't make you a fisherman."

The high, warm sun they had enjoyed all day was slipping fast behind the mountains to the west. Neither the hatch, nor the feeding activity of the trout had slowed, but Jack had as the exchange of ideas circulated in his head.

He was exhausted, more than just physically, mentally, emotionally, spiritually too he thought, though he did not know what that fully meant.

Jack kept envisioning himself like a mason jar whose wide mouth lid had been unscrewed and taken off, and the free flow of ideas coming in and out was pouring in through the top of his head. This day, from start to finish had been like no other he had ever experienced.

"You're right Stu, your meaning of what it means to be a fisherman is accurate for sure." Jack looked at Stu who was amazingly still casting. "I'm beat," he yelled as Stu's cast landed on the water like a feather. In the diminishing light of the day that size eighteen fly was almost invisible. Stu struck sharply as the trout gulped the fly from the surface and the line came flying back past his head.

"Missed him by that much," Stu said in his best Maxwell Smart impression, laughing out loud with a bellow that seemed deeper than should have come from a man of such slight build. He tipped his cap in thanks to the river, the trout, and the day.

"I'm starving" Jack proclaimed as Stu arrived, "I have a couple cold beers and a steak big enough for both of us in the cooler back at the truck. Why don't we head back and make camp in the parking lot?"

"I don't have anything to add to the celebration, and I certainly don't want to impose."

"Impose?" Jack said, looking a little perplexed, "We're friends now; there is no imposition amongst friends, especially fishing friends. Besides, after all that you have shared with me today, the least I could do is repay you with a little food and drink."

"When you put it that way, I accept"

Once back at the parking lot, Stu went to his car and drove it over next to Jack's truck and parked it. Stu pulled out a folding lawn chair from the trunk and set it next to Jack's. The lantern hanging from the open cap door cast a glow fifteen feet out from the back of the truck. At its outer edge, the darkening of the night hung like black-out curtains all around them.

The camp stove was already going with a pan on it. The smell of onions and garlic sautéing filled the air like Sunday at an Italian grandmother's house. Fin was licking his bowl clean from his dinner while waiting patiently behind Jack just in case anything fell to the ground for him.

"I have not smelled anything that good in what seems like a lifetime," Stu proclaimed. "Food cooked outdoors always tastes better, and food after a successful day on the water tastes the best."

"I agree," Jack said, handing Stu a cold beer. The unmistakable sound of the tops being popped rang out in the quiet night, pssscht, pssscht. Jack started to say something as Stu interrupted him.

"This moment reminds me of something an old friend of mine named Henry once wrote in his journal. He was a young man about the same age as you Jack, who was equally full of questions, and searching for his own answers. He learned how to be quiet one day and truly observe and listen to life around him and his role in it, and this is what he said he heard. **'I am disappointed and surprised to find out that men lay so much stress on the fish which they catch or fail to catch, and on nothing else, as if there were nothing else to be caught.**'(Henry David Thoreau journal entry September 26, 1853) "He told me that after a day of excellent fishing we had enjoyed on a little pond named Walden near his house after not catching a thing all day."

Those words seemed very familiar to Jack in the moment for some unknown reason, but he didn't focus on them long before his whole body tingled as the words Stu spoke sunk in. It felt like waves of electricity that were crashing on his shore. This feeling that Jack had never felt before had become common in the last 24 hours. Over and over it happened as his instincts were telling him to accept the feeling as validation of what was said, or what he thought as being true, like a yes answer to a question.

"Look at us now Stu. Even though we had a great afternoon of fishing, amazing really, this moment now, sharing time, talking, communing, is as important to me as the catching was, if not more so. Maybe your friend Henry was right, maybe it was not the fish I was after to begin with?"

Stu only smiled at Jack as he spoke and rolled his right hand in the air signaling him to continue with his train of thought.

"Maybe it is all the aspects of fishing wrapped together, the spot, the time, the learning curve and the success?"

"Continue my boy"

"*Maybe* it is the fact that I was able to share the experience with someone? My fondest fishing memories are with Gramp, or my buddies. That can't be coincidence. That has to be the **more** that he was talking about**?** More than just fish I seek, it is companionship, camaraderie, sharing of time and place. You were right all along Stu, I had to get out of my own way, to be patient and kind with myself, to love myself enough to…"

The crashing vibrations were back so strongly this time that it would not let Jack finish his sentence. He took immediate note of it and stopped speaking. What did Stu say hours ago when they started fishing that resonated so deeply. Was it that he had to be patient and kind with himself? There was no internal response to that. Was it that I had to love myself? The cymbals and waves crashed and vibrated throughout Jack's body. He looked at Stu who was smiling back at him.

"Looks like you might be on to something boy," Stu said as he took a sip of beer. "Don't give right or wrong a second thought, accept that your first thoughts are instinctual *and* true."

Jack let those words sink in like a soft, warm summer rain on a backyard garden. Stu's words were meant to help him grow and he was realizing it in this moment.

"Do you mind if I man the grill while you keep talking?" Stu interjected, "I have not cooked in ages and I miss it."

"Of course not, be my guest; the steak is seasoned and ready to go on. I'm going to sit and drink this beer and digest our conversations for a while as my legs seem a little weak all of a sudden."

Stu chuckled at Jack's feigned disability as the sizzling sound of meat hitting a hot grill took over the conversation.

After an extended silence Jack spoke. "She wanted me to move back at the end of my first enlistment, back to NY where she felt I belonged," Jack mused aloud as he stared directly at the top of the beer can he was holding tightly in his hand, "but I chose to exercise my free will and independence and I reenlisted instead."

"She died the night that I told her my plans. The weight of guilt I feel over this is still unbearable. I replay everything about that time repeatedly in my head, trying to find a way to undo it, to turn back the clock." Jack looked up from the beer can at Stu, his face illuminated from the sheen of tears on his cheeks. "I stopped living that day, I was fucking crushed, and it's all my fault."

Certain moments in life had forever changed Jack and in his mind, there was no going back. Their ripples echoed across him like the aftermath of a rock being tossed into a glassy pond, shattering its tranquility, and it seemed like only yesterday to him that the rock had smashed the glassy surface of his life at twenty-three years old when his grandmother died.

"It's not your fault Jack."

"I killed her Stu; she died that night of a broken heart," Jack sobbed.

Stu left the grill and grabbed the other chair and put it directly in front of where Jack was sitting. Sitting down he patted Jack's knees in a comforting gesture and looked him straight in the eye and said, "I assure you, just like the sun will rise tomorrow, that NONE of this was your fault, you had nothing, and I repeat, nothing to do with her death. Nor do they want you to feel like it is, for even one more second!"

CHAPTER NINE

Two tin plates, two plastic forks, and a very sharp pocketknife that was passed back and forth between the two men were all that was needed to devour the meal of steak and potatoes. Stu's oohing and ahhing with every bite were the only sounds, and it sounded like his first and last meal in a very long time, but unquestionably he was enjoying it.

Jack had so many things going on in his head as he ate, and Stu's proclamation that it wasn't his fault had made him feel surprisingly better. He took the last long sip of beer and looked up at the night sky, bedazzled with millions of tiny flickering diamonds. The beauty of its infinity stretched over big sky country like a blanket that made him feel small in comparison, but comforted that he was not alone.

His head hung back over his chair, eyes fixated on the flickering stars. Jack had always wondered what else there was to this life beyond what he could readily see, and in the last two weeks his eyes had seen unimaginable things. He desperately wanted to know if they were all right, together, and happy. He wanted to be able to communicate again with the two most important people in his life. He had always thought if he could break the code to cross realms that he would not feel so alone anymore without them.

Terrified by the "what if this was it" proposition that physical death without the possibility of resurrection or reincarnation posed in his mind, Jack thought reconnecting with them would prove to his logical mind beyond any doubt that there in fact was life after death. This, he believed, would cure his fear of death and free him from the prison of grief he had sentenced himself to.

The sounds of enjoying a meal had ceased and Stu adjusted himself in his chair after setting the plate on the ground and picking his can of beer back up as he began to speak.

"The spark that is creativity, life, and birth comes from somewhere Jack, so logically, at the time of death, that same energy or spark must go somewhere. If it can ignite and cross realms of physical reality at birth, then it should be able to continue to the next reality after the physical body the energy inhabited has expired."

"You never cease to amaze me, old man. I was just thinking about that very same thing," Jack said nonchalantly.

"It's like miracles," Stu said, "if you believe in one, no matter how small, then by default you have to believe in them all. A miracle is a miracle, no matter the size."

"I see where you're going with this, but give me an example?"

"Ok, for instance, you say you've seen your dead grandparents and it frightened you, but you still admitted that you saw them. It does not matter what your reaction to the miracle was, what matters is that you experienced a miracle by seeing them. So, ipso facto, by connecting those dots then there must be life after death or else you never would have been able to see them because there would be nothing of them left to exist to see."

"It's funny that you put it that way because, up until very recently, I have always proclaimed to the universe that I do not believe unless you show me undeniable proof, a sign, a modern-day burning bush. Show me the sign that meets my criteria, or I am going to stay right here, treading water in the current of despair, frightened and alone, in spite of myself!"

"You set an expectation of yourself and your grief, and when you did not live up to this expected level of grief, you prostrated yourself upon the sword of guilt, cutting out anything and everything that would bring you joy and happiness. How could you be so sure that your beloved grandparents, who loved you unconditionally in life, were now in death sitting in judgement over your every action. Doesn't that seem misguided?"

"One thing is becoming clear Stu. I've sat locked in this "cell" of mine for twenty years now, grieving, blaming himself, and never having said a word to anyone about it until today, and none of it was ever my fault." The vibrations returned as the truth of that statement rang out and Jack felt the chains wrapped around him begin to melt away.

"They were dead. They could no longer feel joy, so I decided if I felt joy, then I was somehow not honoring them? I chose to stay entrenched in mourning because I was sure that was what they wanted and demanded of me. If I didn't, it meant that they were disappointed in me for not honoring their memory well enough, or long enough, or deeply enough."

"Jackie, my boy, your life has become increasingly superficial in ways that have blocked your real emotions or connections. You have spent your time and effort on things designed to distract you from thinking about the future instead of progressing into the future that is in your best and highest good. We talked about deterring the flow of the current, but you've taken that to a whole new level; you have completely obstructed it."

"Talking to you has opened up," Jack paused as a star shot across the night sky, "well, it's opened me up."

"Jack, my boy, we write our own scripts, life is what we ourselves create, and that then makes us responsible for everything that happens to us. I want to truly thank you for dinner tonight, for our day together, and for our conversation tonight, it means a lot to an old ghost like me."

Jack could feel his face smiling as he continued staring at the stars while listening to Stu's words.

"Well you certainly have the old part correct, but I can't speak to the ghost part."

"Just remember my words when I'm gone, boy."

Everything Stu said was bouncing around in Jack's head, he began to say there was no need for thanks when the words Stu spoke became clear and stuck like an arrow hitting the bullseye in his mind.

Jack snapped his head up. "What did you just say? I know those words!" His eyes searched frantically but found nothing. There was no Stu, no chair, no plate, no car, no nothing. He was gone, and Jack was sitting all alone in the night.

The vibrations rang through Jack's body like a fierce summer thunder storm ripping trees from the ground and tearing out power poles. "What the fuck just happened?" he screamed into the darkness.

On his feet now, frantically scanning three hundred and sixty degrees, searching for anything in the black void, tears streaming down his face and hysterical panic in his eyes, the once comforting blanket of night had turned into a suffocating tunicate as he screamed out in agony into the emptiness.

"Stuuuuu!"

CHAPTER TEN

Jack sat perfectly still in the chair for hours in a state of shock. The darkness that was kept at bay last night while sharing a meal with Stu was now inside having completely taken over like an unwelcomed house guest with its feet on the coffee table. The suffocating pressure, the fear of the unknown, the emptiness, were all clawing at his insides now that he was alone again.

He purposely isolated himself and his thoughts. He had never married, had no relationships whether romantic or friendly to speak of. It had always been this way for Jack; he had his grandparents when he was young and now, he had Fin - that was until yesterday, when Stu had come along.

Stu disarmed Jack and seemed to circumvent the barrier walls that had kept everyone out of his life. They had had the deepest and most meaningful conversation in the fleeting period they had been together that Jack had had since his gramp had died. This man that he had met in the parking lot had become his closest friend in a matter of twelve hours, and now inexplicably he was gone without a trace of ever being there in the first place.

Jack could not make heads nor tails of what had happened over the last twenty-four hours, or what had happened weeks ago on the bank of the river. He maddingly replayed both the events non-stop in his mind trying to make sense of it all.

The sound of a vehicle and the clanking of a drift boat bouncing on a trailer as it made its way down the dirt road stirred Jacks senses and drew his attention away for the second morning in a row. He heard the vehicle come to a stop, doors opening and closing, and hushed voices off in the distance.

The sky was faintly starting to lighten in the east as sunrise was on its way to vanquish the darkness from the landscape once again like a valiant knight riding off to fight in the crusades, but Jack knew his internal darkness was not going to fade away anytime soon.

Fin jumped to his feet quickly like he had been startled as the tentative and questioning word, "Hello," pierced the silence of the pre-dawn morning. Jack stood and spun with catlike quickness, as excitement and relief filled his mind and body.

"Stu! You're back!" Jack's eyes met a man's face, but it was not Stu. This face was framed with long dark hair and a greying beard.

"No, it's Dave. I'm a Guide. I'm sorry if I startled you."

Jack had not been able to catch his breath or say a word yet. He could not dismiss the horrible feeling of disappointment he felt deep inside when the voice turned out to not be Stu.

Dave reached his hand down and gave Fin a few pets on the head, saying he had seen Jack yesterday morning as well when he launched his boat, "I saw the New York plates on your truck, and I am originally from New York, so I thought I would come over and introduce myself. You were talking to someone at the back of your truck and I didn't want to interrupt." Dave looked up from petting Fin and made eye contact with Jack and said, "Now this morning, I pull in and find you sleeping in the chair out in the open under the stars."

"Wait" Jack blurted as he was still rubbing the sleep out of his eyes. "You saw me yesterday morning? Talking to someone?"

"Yes" Dave answered, unsure why Jack seemed startled by what he had just said. "You were both standing by the tailgate of your truck when I pulled in with my clients."

"I'm sorry, I didn't mean to jump at you." Jack knew he couldn't tell him the truth about how the man he saw him talking to yesterday had disappeared right in front of his eyes, he couldn't tell anyone that; they would think he was losing his mind, and he was pretty sure they would be right. "I am a little foggy this morning is all. I had a few too many beers last night after I got off the river and must have passed out in my chair."

Dave gave a hearty belly laugh as Jack explained what had happened, all the while noticing that he was still visibly off balance and assuming it was the lingering effects of the beers from last night.

"Don't worry buddy, you're not the first person, or people for that matter that I have found sleeping or otherwise in this parking lot. This river attracts all types, from dignitaries to degenerates, and the wide-open spaces here in the west lends themselves to people letting their hair down in some peculiar ways; nothing I see out here shocks me anymore."

"I can only imagine." Jack tried to focus and be present in this impromptu conversation so that he did not appear as insane on the outside as he felt on the inside.

"Where are you from in New York?" Dave asked, "I grew up in Ithaca, are you familiar with it?"

"I'm from up north, near Pulaski. I've been through your area a few times but can't say that I know it," Jack responded, as he moved to the back of his truck and began to busy himself in an attempt to shorten a conversation that he was in no mood to have.

Seeing that Jack was shutting the door on the commonality that was the base of their conversation, Dave smiled and said, "Well, it's always nice to meet a fellow New Yorker. I better be going."

"Nice to meet you as well; good luck today."

"By the way, how was your day fishing yesterday?" Dave asked as he started to walk away.

"It was amazing" Jack answered, surprising himself a little that he did not search for the proper descriptive adjective, "It was simply amazing! Beyond anything I could have imagined."

Dave stopped in mid-stride twenty feet away from Jack, turning to face him with the slightest of grins on his face and said, "This river has a way of awakening things inside of us that we did not know were even there; she reveals her secrets with every rising trout if you are willing to stop and listen."

Jack had all he could do not to collapse to his knees as Dave spoke and the vibrations came crashing back out of nowhere, buckling his knees like the weight of an elephant had just been placed on his shoulders.

Jack summoned every ounce of strength and composure he had left and waved his arm at Dave in agreement. "You are right about that." Jack responded half-heartedly. "Have a great day on the river." As Jack's arm dropped Dave was gone and their chance meeting had ended, but the aftermath was boiling inside.

Awakening! That word screamed out in his brain. That was the word he was looking for to describe what he was feeling yesterday after the conversation with Stu. *Holy shit! Stu! Dave had seen him yesterday morning here at the truck with me, that means it actually happened, he was here and I'm not fucking nuts after all.*

Awakening again thundered in his belly. The word slammed back into him with reverberating force like a gong had been struck by a giant. That was the feeling he was experiencing when it felt like someone unscrewed the top of his head. Awakening described it perfectly. He was no longer the deterrent to his own current.

The awakening feeling was getting him out of his own way. It was allowing him to visualize and comprehend the concept of being kind and loving to himself first. The exchanges he had shared with Stu had awakened some deep understanding inside himself, and his ability to think through the new concepts was revealing things that had always wanted to come out and be set free but were trapped in theoretical code that he could not crack.

The needle on Jack's mental RPM gauge was pegged to the redline as his wheels were spinning out of control on the thin ice between reality and insanity where he now found himself.

Thoughts and questions were whizzing by at a speed he could not comprehend, blurring his ability to discern fact from fiction. Dave had validated Stu's existence by saying he had seen him yesterday morning with Jack, so it must have been true, but if it were true, then where did he go?

People did not just vanish without a trace, undetected, right in front of someone. At least if it were a dream, Jack thought, he would not feel so bat-shit crazy right now trying to figure out what had happened. There had to be a logical explanation for all of this.

All things could be explained somehow by applying logic and reason, Jack thought. Even people who saw what they thought were UFO's were told it was sewer gas, reflecting off the city lights, or the power plant, or some bullshit made up story, and boom, they had a logical explanation they could wrap their mind around and let it go. Jack had no such explanation, no matter what scenario he applied, and he could not let it go.

Jack sat forward in his chair, resting his head in his hands, shaking it from side to side slightly. "I must be losing my fucking mind," Jack said aloud, "now I am talking about UFO's, next it will be Bigfoot, and pretty soon I will have myself believing in ghosts. Should I believe in ghosts?" As the words left his lips, the tsunami wave of internal vibrations came crashing down on his head, the images of Stu telling him he was an old ghost, of him sneaking up on him repeatedly, of his ability to say things that he couldn't know, his insight into how Jack thought and what he was thinking at exact moments, of him saying he had not had a meal that good in a lifetime, telling him that his grandparents were the nicest people he had ever met, and of the last thing he said to Jack, just before he disappeared, about writing our own scripts.

Jack shuttered at that last thought because what Stu had said had gotten lost the instant he vanished. It had switched Jack's focus which was now aimed back at those words. He leaned back in his chair and reached into his right front pocket pulling out his old brown leather wallet. He opened the wallet and pulled out a three by five-inch piece of paper with quotes written on it. The paper was laminated on both sides and folded in thirds down to the size of a business card.

Jacks grandfather had given him this laminated card many years ago and Jack had kept it tucked in his wallet since that day. Jack never asked where he had found those quotes, or who had originally said them, or why his Gramp had found them important or meaningful enough to write down and give to him. He simply had accepted it, tucked it in his wallet, and kept it with him to read from time to time when he needed inspiration.

Just the comfort of seeing Gramp's handwriting on the piece of paper was usually enough to quell any rising tide of grief Jack was feeling when the realization that he was gone forever was too much to bear.

There were four things hand written by him on the card: One, "we are each the authors of our own lives, there is no way to shift the blame, and no one else to accept the accolades." Two, "the secret of life is too endure." Three, "to excel: stand tall and be strong of heart." The first one that was written on the top of the little paper read, "We write our own scripts, life is what we ourselves create, and that then makes us responsible for everything that happens to us."

Stu had said exactly what was written on the piece of paper, word for word right before he disappeared. Tears blurred Jack's eyes and streamed down his face as he spoke aloud again even though there was no one there but the dog to hear him.

"Please, someone tell me what all of this means; I don't understand, and I don't know what I'm supposed to think. Is any or all of this real?"

Jack called out, and instantly the internal vibrations rang out in him. "Am I crazy?" he said next, and there was nothing. Jack stopped in his tracks as the internal vibrations were replaced by chills running up and down his spine with a revelation that was starting to formulate in his mind.

"Am I getting answers to direct questions?" the vibrations rang through his body once again. "Is someone here with me now?" And the waves of vibrations came crashing back like heavy surf onto a beach.

"Holy shit!" Jack screamed as he lunged upright to attention, knocking his chair back away from him to the ground in the process. Jack shook his arms wildly at his side like an injured bird trying to regain flight in an effort to stop the vibrating feeling that now seemed to be a frequent occurrence inside of him. He walked frantically in circles like something was chasing him where he had just sitting moments before; Jack yelled out again, "What the fuck is going on with me?"

CHAPTER ELEVEN

Jack left the dirt parking lot and turned onto the pavement outside of Fort Smith with dust flying and rubber squealing. The river and the events that had taken place there were in his rear-view mirror now, and he intended to keep them there for his own sanity's sake. He wanted to be out of his head, to stop thinking about eternity, infinity, his soul, and any other souls that may have been around him at the moment.

Fear of the unknown and anger he directed at himself over being scared of that unknown had mixed into a volatile cocktail. Jack put both hands around the steering wheel, gripping it tightly as the veins popped out of the top of his hands as he shook the wheel slightly. His emotions were a mass of confusion as he began to accept what was happening to him.

Stu was one of a very select few people to whom he had ever opened up and connected with. He seemed to understand how Jack's mind worked, whether he was real or not, but then he had vanished. It hurt even worse because he missed Stu and now he was alone again. A familiar albeit uncomfortable position.

He turned onto the westbound ramp of I90 and slid in disc one of the Dead's 1978 Winterland show box set as the familiar opening notes of "Sugar Magnolia" come careening out of the speakers in the truck, "Sugar Magnolia, blossoms blooming, heads all empty and I don't care."

"I *don't* care!" Jack proclaimed to himself before picking up the beat and starting to sing along. "I don't care one fucking bit!" The beat was undeniably strong as always, and it swept Jack off.

"Sugar Magnolia" slipped into a "Scarlet Begonia/Fire on the Mountain" that was just scorching. There was no warm up in this show Jack thought as he drove, and the intensity of the music flowed out of the speakers and into Jack.

He played the drums and did the driver's seat dance for well over an hour as the music played. Jack looked into the passenger seat for the other discs only to find they had slid to the other side of the seat and out of easy grabbing distance. Jack muttered an obscenity or two under his breath, then looked over his shoulder at Fin in the back seat and screamed at the top of his lungs. "Shiiiiit!!!" as his eyes met Stu's sitting in the back seat with the dog.

"You are never alone Jack unless you choose to be," Stu said with a smile.

The heavy percussion crescendo in the apex moment of "Terrapin Station" mixed with the truck tires vibrating on the rumble strips pounded Jack's attention away from the rearview mirror and back to the windshield as he violently jerked the truck after drifting across two lanes of traffic. Once he straightened the truck out, he immediately scanned the backseat again for Stu. There was no one there.

Jack looked over at the center console of the truck as he caught his breath and pulled out one of the freshly-rolled joints that was standing up inside the can. He rolled up the windows and lit it. As he pulled the first puff deep into his lungs, he realized that this was his second smoke of the day just to calm his fraying nerves.

Jack pulled off at the first exit moments later when he saw the beginning of a lake. After twenty minutes he came upon a spot and pulled in down the dirt road a hundred feet off the highway. The drop was steep down to the water's edge, maybe fifteen feet. Jack unstrapped the kayak from the cap of the truck and set it on the ground to load with fishing rods, cooler, and backpack. "Anything else you can think of Fin?" Jack asked as he looked down at the dog who was watching him pack.

The ruck was lashed to the front of the kayak now just like the cooler was in the back with bungee cords of every color. Jack slid the paddle into the cockpit along with the two fishing rods and started to pull the Beverly Hillbilly looking contraption down the path toward the water.

Jack arrived at the cliff and decided that he would stay on top and lower the kayak down the descent, instead of being below the kayak, in case it picked up speed as it came down. The plan seemed solid to Jack, and he started to lower the whole thing down. As soon as the kayak crested the edge it rolled onto its side under the top-heavy weight of the load. When it breached, the bungee cords had given way and the cooler had broken free from its moorings and had slammed down the fifteen-foot rock face before landing at the bottom near the water's edge.

As the cooler went, so did the rucksack, ripping free under its own weight from the cords that bound it, hitting both rods in the cockpit and nearly breaking them as it careened down and joined the cooler at the bottom of the drop off. The primordial scream of "motherfucker, cocksucker, son of a bitching piece of shit!" sprang effortlessly from Jack's lips as he threw an adult version of a tantrum that any five-year-old would be envious of. "You dumb fucking asshole! How can you be so stupid?" The verbal tirade was swift and merciless. Jack was left breathless when it was over. He stood there looking over the edge, still holding the handle on the bow of the kayak.

Stu's voice suddenly whispered in his right ear. "Give yourself a break, be patient and kind to yourself, love yourself for once."

Jack spun around like a flash to try and see the face again that spoke those words but there was no one there. It made Jack stop and think though, *if something like this had happened to a young private under my command during a maneuver, I would have never yelled at him and berated him like I just did to myself, ever. So why am I so quick to do it to myself?* Jack had no answer to his internal question.

Jack took a deep breath and continued to lower the now lighter kayak down the grade until the point of the stern touched the ground next to where the cooler and ruck were lying. Jack climbed the rest of the way down and got the kayak into the water where he reloaded and secured the cargo again front and back.

Fin was playing in the water like a puppy, splashing around and looking for subsurface playmates. Jack pulled the paddle out of the cockpit and carefully got in alongside the fishing rods. With two scoots of his butt and one push with his paddle he was floating free in the lake. He paddled slowly out and around the point to get a better look at his surroundings and the shoreline.

On the far side of the bay he saw a stretch of shoreline that would get the morning sun and where he would be able to see the evening sunsets. There was nothing resembling a dwelling anywhere in sight, so he set off paddling in that direction. Jack heard a yip and then a splash behind him as Fin was not going to be left alone. "Come on, boy, I'll wait for you," Jack yelled back at the dog who was now swimming effortlessly out to meet him.

CHAPTER TWELVE

After the mile and a half paddle across the open water of the bay, the heavily loaded kayak and the four-legged doggie paddling virtuoso arrived at the far shore. Fin immediately exited the water and started running back and forth along the steep shoreline, sniffing, inspecting, and peeing on everything in sight.

Jack laughed at his companion's antics and admired his endless energy and enthusiasm. His whimsy and abandon were that of a curious puppy, and from a distance his gait appeared to be that of a dog only a year or two old, but upon closer inspection you see the face that time had decorated with knowledge, wisdom, and with silvery highlights on his chin, muzzle, and eyebrows.

Thirty feet in front of him as he paddled, he could see there was a large spruce tree that had lost its battle with wind, erosion, and verticality. It was now horizontal with half of its branches beneath the surface and the other half protruding upward out of the water like the spine of a sea serpent.

The fallen tree was covering the entrance to a small cove off the main bay. It revealed the secret it was hiding to Jack only because he is paddling so close that he could see through it. It was like finding a treasure or an oasis in a desert, Jack thought to himself, and he quickly slipped his kayak behind the curtain of green and brown that was standing guard.

Once inside the perimeter of the cove Jack saw a small flat beach and he knew he had found a home for the next couple of days. The shoreline of the beach was dotted with fallen trees and logs bleached by the sun. One log lay parallel to the water and served perfectly as a backrest when sitting and watching the fire at night.

Jack started scavenging for fire wood. It was like policing the grounds around the barracks for Jack, and he would burn anything and everything he could find lying about. When he was gone, he thought to himself, no one would even see the pile of ashes where the fire was; there would be no trace of him ever having been here.

That thought immediately struck a chord with him as soon as he had said it, "When I am gone from this body and this earth, there will be no trace of me left behind either; there's no one to remember me, I will cease to exist, I will be no more."

Chills gripped Jack, and his stomach tightened as the words sank in. Jack shook his head violently trying to erase what he had just said in an effort to keep the crippling fear of his own death at bay, but no matter how hard he shook, the feeling would not go away. The darkness of death enveloped Jack, the silence deafening, it gripped him and didn't let go.

He had only ever dealt with two deaths in his life, and they were the two most important people in his world, his grandparents. He had never been able to accept, come to grips with their passing, or move on from his grief over it, and now he was thinking about what his own passing would be like.

Jack's sense of loss had kept him isolated, unable to feel joy out of guilt that he was alive, and they were not. It was a twisted sense of survivor's remorse that he employed to purposely sabotage his own life. He had spent countless hours and days wishing for just one more moment to spend with them, to somehow see them again.

"Then I suddenly do see them, or at least I think I did, and it scared the ever-loving shit out of me."

Jack mumbled to himself as he walked the beach still collecting fire wood. "I have spent my whole life asking questions that I have never gotten answers to, and now when I think I might be getting answers directly from the source, it is spooking me so much that I am trying to distract myself and not think about any of it. I spent the most amazing day talking and fishing with a man who was wise, patient, and filled with love. Why then, when he was gone, was I filled with anger and terror over that encounter?"

"Are the vibrations that I feel inside of me *really* indicating a Yes response to a question that I ask?" The vibration landed on Jack's head with such force that he dropped the sticks he had collected bringing him to his knees right where he stood. Jack was kneeling on the shore of a picturesque lake twenty-five hundred miles from home and somehow, someway, for what-ever reason, he was being shown a gift that allowed him to talk directly with whatever was beyond what he could see.

CHAPTER THIRTEEN

The symphony of squawking seagulls and honking Canadian geese greeted the new day joyfully and without regard for anyone who wished to sleep through their daily sunrise salutation. There was no place to hide from the clamor of sounds out in the bay just past the evergreen fence at the end of the cove, so Jack opened his eyes, sat forward, and stretched his arms high and wide, letting out a deep guttural growl that a big Papa Lion would have been proud of.

Jack took a moment to survey his surroundings. Everything was just as he left it, including the food that he had cooked and left on the grill. Jack looked at the two hockey puck burgers that were pitch black beyond recognition and couldn't remember when he had even started to cook them.

The sight of food instantly made his stomach growl with the realization that he had not eaten any dinner last night and that he was now starving as the morning sun peeked above the ridge line behind him.

Jack's heart immediately filled with anticipation over one of his favorite things, campfire breakfast. Bacon, eggs, and potatoes mixed with wood smoke and lake water coffee are the things dreams were made of, Jack chuckled to himself, at least his dreams anyway.

Jack got up from his wooden couch and built the tee pee of tinder sticks around the hot embers to get the campfire hot enough to cook on. Within minutes the fire was breathing on its own and no longer required Jack's constant attention to stay alive. Fire was a living, breathing thing, Jack thought, as he continued to stare. If you gave it what it truly desired, then the flames would grow and flourish as they were intended to do. Jack looked at the dancing flames while simultaneously the theories in his mind frolicked along and the two entities coordinated on the same rhythm.

"I love this fire" Jack said aloud. "I love it for what it is, as well as loving it for what I need it for. I am allowing the fire to be what it is intended to be, a fire, and I am nurturing it to be the best fire that it can be. Strong, hot, and focused by placing kindling and then larger sticks in such a way that it can breathe and grow but not burn out of control and then extinguish itself."

"The fires purpose with a directed flame is to super heat the skillet that I will cook my breakfast on. My loving actions toward it allows the fire to be fulfilled in its purpose and allows me to use its natural flow to my benefit as well. I love and respect myself and the fire, I can help the fire be what it is meant to be; I can also utilize the fire and its natural byproduct for what I need. It is a symbiotic relationship based in loving reverence for self and others."

Jack knew as he said the words aloud that his thoughts were correct in theory and that this path of thought was important, life changing even, but a bit corny sounding. He was amazed though at the clarity, insight, and articulation he had found in the last couple of days. The last couple of days since he met Stu was what he truly meant, everything about his thinking had changed.

"I need food, fun, and to give my mind a rest from everything that is going on in there." The sun was not fully up in the sky yet as Jack watched Fin drink from the crystal-clear waters of the lake. "It certainly is beautiful here, Boy" Jack said to Fin. As he was talking, he saw rings on the water by the fallen tree.

There were trout sipping their breakfast off the surface and quickly a lure was tied on one of the rods as Jack walked toward the fallen tree to get a better casting angle to the rising trout. As he made his first cast, he swore he heard his gramps voice encouraging him to be prepared for the strike. Jack looked as if he was going to see him standing there; when he didn't, a feeling of melancholy washed over him.

The tiny lure hit the water barely causing a ripple. Jack was still half-heartedly looking around for the origin of the voice, when it dawned on him, go ahead and ask. Jack was amazed that the thought had come to his mind, amazed that he thought he could communicate with something, whatever it was, amazed that the desire to talk to his beloved grandfather was stronger than the fear he felt after seeing him unexpectedly.

Jack summoned courage from deep within himself, pushed the melancholy aside and asked the words aloud. "Gramp are you here?" The thunderous vibrations rang down from the heavens proclaiming the one he had loved and lost, may not be lost after all.

"OMG! Are you really here with me?" The vibrations rang true again. Jack's poor bewildered mind was blown wide open once again. Tears filled his eyes until reality slapped him back as the little ultra-light rod slammed in his hand and then doubled over under the weight of a fish.

It zigged and zagged in frenzied fashion and even jumped once showing Jack it was a proud and fierce rainbow trout sixteen inches long. When the fight subsided Jack slid the trout onto the shore where it lay still for a moment so that Jack could admire the violet purple stripe on its side that went from its cheek to its tail and the thousands of black spots that covered over the silvery skin that shimmered in the water like a freshly minted nickel.

"Do you see what I caught, Gramp?" The vibrations rang true inside of Jack. "If you are here, is Gramma here with you too?" The vibration resonated again feeling like it was twice as strong. Tears again started to flow down Jack's cheeks. "That makes me so incredibly happy to know that you are both together."

The questions started to formulate like rising flood waters and Jack could not ask them quickly enough before five more became known. "Where are you? What is it like there?" No response to those questions.

Wait! Jack said to himself. *I have to remember that it is only yes or no questions.* "I miss you both very much, every single day. It has been so hard for me since you both have left; I have felt so alone without you. I cannot believe that I am actually talking to you right now. I am having a hard time believing anything these last couple of days. I met a man named Stu who said he knew you, he opened my eyes to things that are very hard for my logical mind to accept. At first Gramp, I thought you were Stu, were you Stu?"

No vibration. That was not the response Jack anticipated. "Do you know Stu?" The vibration returned a yes answer.

"Did you send him?" No vibration again. Jack was talking and thinking so fast that he was out of breath and unable to continue.

The fish flopped on the edge of the water and drew Jack's attention. If anyone was watching him from afar for the last twenty minutes, they would think he was completely and certifiably nuts. They would have seen him talking to a fire, a dog, and to himself, while crying over a fish and wandering back and forth along the shore line waving his arms like he was trying to fly.

Thank goodness the tree at the mouth of the cove provided privacy for his antics, he thought. He did not have to be embarrassed because there was absolutely no one around to see him or judge him. Secretly though, Jack was sure that he was losing his mind and slipping into the depths and unhinging from reality.

"Hey Gramp, I have an idea. How about bacon-wrapped trout and eggs for breakfast?" The vibration returned, but this time it danced with a speed and intensity that felt like excitement. Jack acknowledged his grandfather's anticipation of fresh trout cooked over an open fire, and for breakfast no doubt. "How decadent are we," he would have said. What he really would have said Jack thought, and what he said all the time in these types of situations was, "I wonder what the poor people are doing today?"

It took Jack until later in life to realize what he meant when he said that phrase. He meant that even in the humblest of experiences he was mindful enough to appreciate them and he felt rich beyond belief. The joke was, he felt rich in spirit and those people who were unable to be mindful and appreciative were poor in spirit.

Fin met him half way after he noticed the boss was carrying something and he dashed to him to inspect his catch. Fin bounced like his legs were made of coil springs when he was happy or excited about something, and he was both of those things right now. He sniffed and licked the fish in between bounces until Jack was forced to tell him enough, and to calm down, "I love you, dog," Jack said, "but you make me crazy sometimes."

Jack quickly cleaned the fish and rinsed it in the lake. The trout had sliced onion, three strips of raw bacon and some pepper stuffed into the cavity and had been placed skin side down directly on the hot cooking grate. The potatoes and the trout had cooked in about the same time and given the grumbling of Jack's stomach wasn't a moment too soon.

Jack sat on the ground admiring the improvised table he had made that was covered with food. When it was over, the kayak table looked like a buffet line that thirty starving soldiers had destroyed. The trout had been picked clean and there were only the skin and bones left to know it existed at all. The golden yellow remains of the brown farm eggs were as vibrant a color as the sun itself as he stared at the deep rich color of their yolks that looked like the origin of life.

Jack sat back and looked at his surroundings, scratched the chin of his best friend, then turned his voice skyward and said, "I wonder what the poor people are doing today, Gramp?"

CHAPTER FOURTEEN

The late afternoon sun was strong and hot, and Jack had sweat through his t-shirt hours ago.

"Let's take a swim and maybe I'll wash my ass, so I don't smell like a wild animal anymore." Jack sat down on the log couch and pulled his hiking boots and socks off as he dug his feet into the sand, crunching it between his toes. He opened the Yeti can and pulled out a pre-rolled joint and lit it. Pulling the smoke heavy into his lungs, exhaling, puffing, repeating. The joint would help numb some of the pain that the cold-water bath he was about to jump into would cause, Jack rationalized to himself.

Standing now, he stripped off his shorts and underwear and grabbed his soap. The feeling of being naked in the outdoors was both liberating and humbling, making him feel connected and vulnerable simultaneously.

Movement on shore caught his attention and he froze like a statue as he stared back at the shoreline and his fire pit. His eyes blinked once and then again in an attempt to process what he was seeing as a long-legged, green-eyed brunette had suddenly appeared out of nowhere and was walking toward him. He squinted this time to try and focus his bloodshot eyes and make sure what he was seeing was actually there. The woman continued toward him.

He did not recognize the lines of her face as she smiled at him while returning his gaze. She continued to saunter toward him as her demeanor began to smolder with every seductive step. Jack watched in awe as the chestnut-haired siren began to strip off her clothes like a model walking down the runway. Jack could not summon any words as his hands began to sweat, his breath started to quicken, and his gaping mouth dried out in the summer heat.

He watched as each of her steps was placed directly in front of the other exaggerating the sway of her hips with every stride. Her perfect toes pointed directly at him as she walked. The blood coursed through his body like it was being pumped by a jet engine, engorging his exposed flesh into a thickened, tingling, throbbing mass.

This unknown vision before him was naked now as she continued to close the distance between them. Jack scanned her entirely from the nape of her neck across to her shoulder, the fullness of her breasts, the darkened shading of her taut nipples, the slight curve of her waist down to her hips attaching her long, elegant legs like those of a dancer. His eyes prepared his body for the first touch of her silken skin to his.

She stood before him as his soldier was rigidly saluting and with a teasing touch she ran her crimson fingertips up his thigh, across his groin, down his shaft and over the tip with a playful flick.

The jolt sent shockwaves across Jack's whole body as he convulsed uncontrollably in anticipated ecstasy. The Sirens ruby red nails continued past his belly button and up his chest, under his chin, across his jaw and over his lips as she stretched on her tip toes and wrapped her arms around his neck, placing her lips feverishly against his.

Time froze as he felt the warmth and pressure of her velvety lips and his arms raised to embrace and draw her closer. The heat of her mouth enveloped his bottom lip as she bit and tugged it, his hands now woven into her hair at the back of her neck, he gripped her and held her tightly in place.

The splash of water on Jack's backside was heart stopping. His eyes scanned frantically only to find Fin already in the water behind him.

The spell was broken, the unknown vision was gone, "Dammit, dog, what have you done?" he exclaimed as he looked down at his chiseled hardness, shaking his head and asking himself who the hell that had been just now.

She was so familiar, he thought, her movements so real and captivating. Her eyes looked inside of him so lovingly that he was still throbbing uncontrollably like a release was about to happen over something that wasn't even real. Shame and embarrassment replaced arousal as the anger welled up inside of him.

"I made this whole thing up, every bit of it, and I am telling you that it stops now. There obviously was no woman just now, and certainly no Stu, or my grandparents sitting on the fucking bench next to me, and I'm completely making up these feelings of vibrations in my head because those aren't real either."

The only thing that was real in this place and time was Fin and I." Jack looked down at Fin who was staring up at Jack; the emotions inside of him were boiling over as he said. "You are the only friend I have, boy, and I think I'm losing my fucking mind! Maybe we should get the fuck out of here and back to the truck? As far away from here as we can possibly be."

CHAPTER FIFTEEN

The end of the cove was completely devoid of light, the fallen tree had absorbed every ray as it drew Jack's eye toward it. He could not help but think it looked like an open gate to what heaven might look like, an illuminated pathway shimmering like a translucent carpet of diamonds, ushering one toward the quiet, peaceful, dark of the night that lay beyond.

"I am in my mid-forties, I have no wife or girlfriend, no kids, no family, no home, no job now, and no God-blessed idea of why I am here or where I am going. I am trying desperately to fight the feelings that I am having a nervous breakdown given the extraordinary events of the last couple of weeks. Hell, I even created a fantasy woman who looked and felt so real that I miss her now and want her back all to combat my loneliness."

Darkness turned to dawn and then to daylight as Jack said his peace while staring blankly at the pure white of the clouds as they drifted lazily along through the azure blue sea above. Something inside of Jack was still not allowing him to accept the immense magnitude of what was transpiring in his life.

It was easy, Jack thought, to ask unanswerable questions, or at least what he might have thought were unanswerable. He never imagined getting an answer, until he got an answer, and found out he was completely unprepared for it, even more unprepared that there was an answer at all.

"Where and who is this answer coming from? I never paid a lot of attention during first communion class," Jack proclaims aloud, "and I have not been to church in over thirty years, so I don't know any reason you would pick me to talk to. I am nobody important, that is for sure."

I have no desire to talk directly to God if there even is a God, and is that even the right name to call it? Is it the Universe? Or some grand Creator of all things? I certainly do not want to offend anyone by calling it, or him, or whatever, the wrong name."

I swear I must be insane, Jack thought at that moment. What would I even say? What could I say that he, or it, would not know already? I would not want to bother him or anyone else up there, if there even is an up there in the first place, with dumb questions.

"This is a perfect example of a time that I wish my grandparents were here with me," Jack said to himself, "to help guide me through this mess and help me sort things out so they made sense." They were my rock, they were who I relied on and they never let me down. They were the only ones I had, considering I never knew who my Father even was, and having a Mother that I was never able to connect with when and if she was around.

Then they died and left me alone to figure everything out for myself, which I clearly have not done a very good job at. I certainly could not tell anyone about what was happening to me. They would lock me up in the nut house for sure. They would say, "Oh, that poor soldier boy is all messed up from the war. He is seeing and hearing things now."

But this had nothing to do with the traumatic experiences he had witnessed during battle; this was all real. As the word real left his lips the vibrations came singing through him once again. Jack stopped in mid-sentence, it was real, wasn't it? Stu was real, the vibrations were real. "I'm not making this shit up" Jack proclaimed aloud to no one as his body felt like a tuning fork.

The sheer beauty of the new day, the bright, warm, late summer morning sun on his back, the clear cloudless blue skies above, and the shimmering lake of diamonds in front of him helped push back the negative feelings that normally percolated within him when faced with change or uncertainty.

Jack was anxious and energized, unable to sit still. He had to busy himself right away or risk back sliding into his own mind, past the progress he had just made to a place where fear of the unknown ruled.

"Do something productive, Jack," he proclaimed to himself in a stern voice and it brought him a burst of activity. He was now hustling around his campsite looking to pack all his belongings and get moving forward, where ever forward might be, as soon as possible.

Free time now would mean time to think deeply and that was not what he wanted right at the moment. Even fishing, his most beloved pass time, would have allowed too much time for reflection and over-thinking. Jack had made the statement that the events were real, and the vibrations reinforced that, so he was not going to go back over it all again and second guess himself.

Jack flipped over the kayak and slid it into the shallow water and began to load his gear onto it. The high wispy white clouds passed over Jack's head and disappeared beyond the cliffs at the back of the cove as he went about his business.

He turned and waded out into the shallows of the sand bar pushing the kayak so that it would float when he got into it. Knee deep in water now he swung his right leg over the transom and slid his butt down into the cockpit. Gathering himself and finding his balance in the water came naturally as he raised his head to begin paddling and there was Stu, standing on shore, right hand raised like an old Indian, smiling at him.

Having someone appear out of nowhere is startling, and this was no different as Jack could feel his breath catch, but he instantly returned Stu's smile with one of his own.

"Jesus, Stu, you have quite the knack for making entrances."

"I know, it's a gift, but I am impressed at how you are getting better at handling the unexpected."

"Very funny. Just a little while ago I thought I was having a nervous breakdown, so the Universe's twisted sense of humor sent me a ghost as reassurance that I'm not crazy!"

Stu, now doubled over in laughter, slapped his thigh as he said, "When you put it that way, you're right, that is pretty funny."

"Ha ha ha laugh it up. I'm trying to be serious here. A lot of shit has happened in the last couple of weeks and I'm struggling to absorb it all, and I might add your random pop ins and outs aren't necessarily helping things either."

Adjusting himself and putting on his best serious face, Stu looked back at Jack. "Boy, you have trained men and lead them into battles, you have basically raised yourself and blossomed into a kind and generous man, so why is it that you think you can't handle the information that you are being shown now? Why do you want someone else to tell you what to do when you already know what to do? Trust that you will act on your behalf, in your best interest."

The jingling sound of tags on Fin's collar caught Jack's attention and he looked to see what the dog was doing, except he wasn't there.

"That's funny… did you just hear Fin?"

There was no answer from Stu.

"STU! Of course, you're gone, why wouldn't you be."

Calling to Fin as he gathered himself again he started to paddle to the end of the cove. There was no sound behind him, no tags jingling on his collar, no splashing sound, all was silent except for the whispering wind through the pines and the soft sound of the water lapping against his kayak.

Jack looked over his shoulder and called for the dog again. Nothing. He was turned completely around now toward shore. There was no sight of black fur anywhere. "Where the fuck did that dog go?" Jack said aloud as he called for him again, this time with more volume. "Herrrrreeee Boyyyy!"

As the echoes of his voice dissipated into the air, the silence returned and there was no sign of Fin anywhere in the cove.

Panicky now, Jack screamed, "Finnnnnnn, HERE!" in the most desperate tone he had ever heard come out of his mouth. Jack was taken back by the sound of his own voice and the desperate tone it took. Fin wandered off all the time, but this time he had just disappeared into thin air.

Jack passed the tree at the end of the cove and out into the open bay in a matter of seconds, scanning the steep shoreline on either side for any sign of his four-legged companion. Panic knotted in his belly as Jack continued to call for the dog.

An hour passed as Jack paddled up and down the lake for miles in each direction screaming at the top of his lungs for his best friend to return. Exhausted from the search, Jack headed back to where the truck was parked in order to call for help. *Maybe,* he thought, *I can get a powerboat somehow, so I can cover more of the lake to look for Fin.*

"I have been so distracted lately," he mumbled, "is that why you ran away, boy? I'm sorry if that's the case. You're all I have. I don't want to be alone."

As he paddled, he heard Stu's words from the backseat of the truck in his head, "You are never alone unless you choose to be."

"Well," Jack said as the nose of the kayak touched the shore where the truck is parked, "I don't choose to be alone without my best friend. I will never stop searching until I find him."

Jack dragged his gear up the hill with weary arms and there was Fin, standing by the truck, wagging his tail. Instantly, Jack lit up like a Christmas tree, dropped his gear, and got down on one knee as relief and joy filled his heart and mind.

Fin uncharacteristically came over to Jack in a very calm and deliberate fashion and nudged his hand gently with his nose as if to say everything was all right.

"Damm it, dog, you scared…" Jack stopped mid-sentence, grabbed the warm pile of black fur, and squeezed him tightly around the neck. "Good boy, such a good boy," he repeated.

The reunion was short but sweet. Jack wiped the tears from his face as he stood up, climbed into the driver's seat and shut the door. He reached for the keys and his hand brushed against the Post-It note taped to the dashboard with the faded yellow color and the faint words on it saying, "30 Days to Divinity." Staring at the words on the paper he could not remember writing them or taping it to the dashboard.

"Are these words important…?" Jack's hesitation melted away as the vibrations indicated that they were.

CHAPTER SIXTEEN

Hours passed as the pleasantly warm sun that shone this morning was gone, replaced now by a burning fireball sitting high in the sky above. With the windows rolled up Jack was still sitting in the cab of the truck with his foot on the brake in front of the two road signs trying to decide which way to go.

He noticed the beads of sweat as they cascaded down his forehead, crossing over his eyebrows and into his eyes with a salty sting as others streamed over his stubbled face that had been left uncut for weeks now.

In his head Jack kept going over the events in order to try to find the answer on which way to go. "Stu is clearly teaching me lessons, lessons which I am gradually understanding; my struggle is taking them from theory to practice," Jack thinks, "but wouldn't it be easier to learn with his full time help rather than just my own?" There was no vibration.

Jack shifted in his seat under the weight of that last question and moved his right foot to help adjust himself. As he lifted his foot the truck began to roll forward; surprised by the movement Jack slammed his foot back onto the brake and shook the cobwebs from his head as he looked around at his surroundings.

"I did not realize the truck was still in drive," Jack said aloud to no one, focusing his eyes on the same two blue highway signs that had been in front of him all day. To the right was a gravel area that adjoined the on-ramp for the east bound highway entrance. The gravel area was large enough that it looked like a tractor trailer could turn around in there or park.

Jack again took his foot off the brake pedal, this time on purpose, and placed it gently on the gas pedal as the truck crawled across the gravel lot, cinders crunching under his tires as it creeped into the back corner where he put the dust covered truck in park and shut off the ignition.

I've been sitting in the truck on the side of the road for almost six hours, Jack thought disgustedly to himself as he looked at his watch. *What the fuck is wrong with me? He said I was never alone unless I chose to be, yet I am alone to make this decision because there is no one else here to help or tell me what to do.*

"I just want to find a place I fit in, where I feel comfortable, where I belong," the words felt like a prayer before communion that were instantly shattered by the bellowing sound of an engine brake on a semi-tractor.

The behemoth had just pulled into the small gravel lot right next to where Jack was parked. When it came to a stop, the driver set his air brakes in the trailer and the tractor produced a loud whoosh sound followed by an elongated high-pitched hiss that sounded like someone had stepped on the tail of a very pissed off snake.

Jack was startled by the noise and shaded now from the shadow cast by the log filled leviathan parked next to him with its payload of sticks stacked ten feet high inside its claw- shaped trailer.

"Dammit, Mister," the driver said to Jack out the now open window, "I had no idea anyone was in the truck when I pulled in and parked right next to you, I'm sorry."

"It's ok, really, I must be getting on the road anyway."

"I'm really sorry; my name is Omar." as he extended his hand out to shake.

"It's ok, like I said, I have to get on the road anyway," as he returned the hand shake.

"Where are you headed? I can see from those New York plates that you are already a long way from home."

"I'm trying to figure out where I'm headed as well," Jack replied as he looked away, "I'm kind of at a proverbial fork in the road as we speak."

Omar laughed uncomfortably in response to what Jack had said, louder than what he should have, now realizing he was not joking. "Sorry, I thought you were joking about the fork."

"It's ok, I guess a grown man, twenty-five hundred miles from home and not knowing where he is going is pretty funny if you think about it." as Jack now found himself smirking at the notion.

"It is a beautiful spot here," Omar astutely said to change the subject and avoid further embarrassment for Jack, "I stop here all the time on this run."

"Where are you headed? Jack asked in retort, "and I bet you have a better answer than I do."

As Jack asked the question, he looked at the door of the tractor to see where the truck was from; in his haste he had read something and something Logging & Trucking, somewhere B.C. This detail was irrelevant as Omar was the first living person he had talked with since the day he had fished with Stu.

Holy shit, Stu! Why was he at the lake, what did he want to talk to me about? Why the fuck, how the fuck had he appeared out of nowhere again?

I still do not know if Stu is actually real, Jack thought to himself, *even though he seemed very real at the time, but then he disappeared into thin air. Then there was the woman on the beach that aroused me and then vanished, and now I wonder if this truck driver is real? Like really real? A living and breathing person? How can I find out for certain?*

"Did you say you stop here in this spot all the time?" Jack asked.

"Yes" Omar replied, "I do this run twice a week during the good weather months."

"What do you do the rest of the year?" Jack asked.

"I'm also the bookkeeper; it's a long story," Omar said as he paused, "but getting out of the office is important for me and the last five years has taken me and my family on quite a journey to where we are now."

Jack was intently watching and listening to Omar, to the words he spoke, his mannerisms, body language, and even the look on his face. This time paying full attention but also surveying him still trying to ascertain if he was real or a figment of his own imagination, like he was now accepting that Stu and the mystery woman had been, not to mention the vision of his grandparents that had started this whole journey.

Jack was okay with accepting that it was all in fact not real and that it had been a figment of his imagination created for some reason. He did not want to investigate any further. Jack nodded to the decision and compartmentalized all of them in that moment and locked them away.

Jack blinked as Omar asked him, "where are you from in New York?"

"I'm from a small town north of Syracuse"

"That's funny, my wife and I have two close friends who met while attending Syracuse University."

Jack smiled at Omar and shook his head as he said how funny the old saying of, "it's a small world" always seemed to be true.

"That is fascinating to me" Jack said to Omar. "I have always thought of our lives as if they were a line traveling across a timeline, every human on the planet has his own line and we are all running parallel to each other. If coincidentally we meet then our lines intersect, join, and move forward together, even if forward is only for the briefest of moments."

Omar openly laughed at Jack and what he had just said, "I will tell you, my new friend, what is really funny; we have only been friends for ten minutes now and we are about to have our first disagreement as I set you straight on the facts of life and how there is no such things as random or coincidence."

The loud thumping sound of a rig with its engine brake engaged coming down the East bound off-ramp of the highway caused Omar to stop mid-sentence as both men turned their heads to see the source of the interruption.

"Continue, please." Jack said, "I want to hear the rest of it, should I pull out the camp stove and make a pot of coffee?"

Omar looked at his watch and smiled, "I would love to, Jack" he said, "but my break is up, and I have to get back on the road, but I would sincerely like a raincheck on the coffee and conversation though." Omar said as he extended his right hand again for a shake.

Jack reached for his hand to shake goodbye this time. Omar unblinkingly looked Jack in the eye as he grasped his hand firmly and said, "If you ever find yourself in Devine, British Columbia, stop by the mill, I will introduce you to everyone, and we can finish this over that cup of coffee."

Jack's blood turned ice cold as he tried to pull his hand free from the grasp and his eyes from the gaze. *What did he just say*? flashed through Jack's mind. *Did he just say Devine was the name of the town where the mill he works at is located?* The vibrational answer of yes reverberated through Jack's entire body and this time he snapped his hand free from Omar's grip. As he backed away, he stared wildly at him as the image of the faded yellow Post-It note taped to the dash board, not more than fifteen feet away in the cab of his truck, was now like a flashing neon sign before his eyes.

"It was great to meet you Jack," Omar said as he turned to walk back to his truck, "remember, buddy, nothing is random, there is no such thing as coincidence, our lines did not intersect today by chance." With a wave, Omar put the truck in gear and pulled away.

CHAPTER SEVENTEEN

Jack stood there staring at the on-ramp after Omar's truck was long out of sight, his thoughts bouncing to and fro inside his head like a ball inside a pinball machine that he was unable to corral and hold still.

Wildly his thoughts, theories and emotions flew by his eyes with great speed, each eliciting a different response or question. Jack was done asking questions because he did not want to know the answers anymore. "Fin!" He yelled out, "here, boy, let's go." There was a moment of caught breath in Jack as the sound of his voice dissipated into silence. Then, faintly, he could hear the tags on Fin's collar jingling together as the dog double-timed his way back over to his side and he exhaled a silent sigh of relief.

Jack whispered softly upon his arrival, "Don't you dare pull a disappearing act on me again, fuck face," as he pet and scratched the black and grey muzzle softly.

Jack closed the door behind his friend and walked around the cab and got in the driver's seat. He reached for his keys on top of the dash and looked directly at the faded yellow Post-It note still taped there.

The chill that ran up and down his spine was noticeably different to Jack. "These words must be a key, I just have to focus on an answer," as he shoved the key into the ignition. Jack was now in the second full day without having anything to eat. His appetite had vanished for the first time in his life, but the smell of the truck stop diner as he stood at the gas pumps beat on his nose like a bacon-wrapped fist.

Jack acknowledged the smell and dismissed it as he then turned his attention internally. There was no hunger pain emanating from his stomach. As Jack did a quick check of the rest of his body's systems, he felt nothing from any of them, nothing was screaming out to him for attention, but none of them was responding either, so this was what completely numb feels like, he thought.

The Pink Floyd song "Comfortably Numb" chorus chimed in his head and was dismissed instantly. *I am not comfortable in any way. I, in fact, am so uncomfortable I do not know what to do with myself or where I should be or go.*

I am free to go anywhere I please for the first time in my life. Jack's thoughts are cut off abruptly by the sound of the pump handle clicking and shutting off that signaled the tank was full.

"Freedom is just another word for nothing left to lose," the great Janis Joplin sang that line while riding across the country with Bobby McGee with no particular destination in mind. The lyric made Jack recall his twelfth grade History teacher Mr. Trager saying that same line to him after asking Jack once what he wanted to do with his life and Jack's response was that he wanted to be "free."

Just one more thing that was falling into place now and suddenly had a deeper meaning, Jack thought, thirty years after the fact, but why now? Jack replaced the handle in the cradle of the gas pump and completed the sale. He looked to the Diner as if to again consider going in for breakfast but changed his mind, "I just want to keep going, keep moving."

As he pulled out of the driveway he was again faced with the same decision from yesterday. "Do I go east or west?" Jack said aloud in the cab. He looked and if he wanted to go east then he had to make a left and go back under the overpass toward the gravel area he had just come from and make another left onto the east bound on-ramp. But, if he wanted to go west he only had to go straight as the west bound on-ramp was directly in front of him where the driveway of the truck stop led out.

I might as well keep going west, Jack said to himself as he crossed the road and headed up the on-ramp. As the truck started up the incline to where the grade of the highway was, Jack got slammed in the chest with a hammering fist of indecision and he abruptly pulled over on the shoulder half way up the ramp.

"The farther west I've gone so far the worse it's gotten for me," Jack again said aloud in response even though he was alone. "I just want this all to stop, maybe it is time to just go home, even though I do not have a home or anyone to go home to, maybe I should just say 'back to the area that I know and am familiar with?"

In an instant, Jack made a one hundred eighty degree turn in his thinking and planning and decided to turn around, tuck tail, and go back to his comfort zone. Jack nodded his head in self-agreement as he came to the decision and hastily grabbed the steering wheel and without looking whipped the truck into a rapid U-turn in the middle of the on-ramp.

As the nose of the truck reached the center of the single lane on-ramp Jack heard the fantastically loud shrill of a tractor trailers air horn vibrating the driver's side window like it was going to explode.

The blaring sound was so loud and close that Jack winced, his eyes instinctively closed, and his body braced for impact as he slammed his right foot deep into the brake pedal. Jack's truck jerked violently forward as its momentum was hastily voided and his seatbelt snapped tight and forced him back in his seat.

The screaming sound of the air horn as it passed inches in front of the hood of Jack's truck continued, and the violently fast thumping of the trailer's driver's side tires going over the rumble strips on the far side of the lane, combined to make up the sound of panic and terror.

The seconds passed like eternity as Jack's eye lids relaxed enough for him to see out from behind them as the blur of pure white from the side of the trailer felt like speeding down an illuminated tunnel as his truck shook when the trailers wind rampaged into its side.

The next split of a second found Jack gripping the wheel with both hands still in position to withstand the force of the inevitable impact which thankfully did not come. There, almost completely broadside on the ramp, Jack's heart raced out of control and his eyes hysterically scanned in both directions as he saw the tail lights of the trailer out his passenger side window crest the on-ramp and disappear out of sight onto the highway above.

The only sound that could be heard inside the cab of the truck was Jack's hyper-ventilated breathing. Jack was hysterical, shaking uncontrollably, and in shock as his fists were clenched around the steering wheel so tightly it felt like they had melted into it. He could see all the way back down the on-ramp where he had come from as his eyes finally responded to his brain telling them to focus. Looking across the road and into the parking lot of the truck stop, there was no traffic in sight. Realization set in that Jack had nearly got himself and Fin killed.

His breathing remained elevated but no longer panicked as the adrenaline slowly ebbed and left his body. Jack's fingertips reached for the lever that turned on the signal light as he started to ease the truck left into the right lane of the highway.

There was little traffic on the west bound side of the road this morning and after the fifth flash of the signal on the dash he had made the lane change and was bringing his truck cautiously up to cruising speed.

Staring straight ahead, still in shock from the near accident moments earlier and the culmination of the events from the past weeks, he muttered repeatedly under his breath, "The truck must be a sign to keep going west."

The beauty of seeing the approaching Cascade Mountains in front of him and then crossing over the top of their spine as Jack made his way down their western slope toward the distant Pacific Ocean was not enough to awaken his senses as the numbness that crept into his bones continued to bore deeper into his being.

He had distant family to the south in Los Angeles; to the north was blank to him. He knew somewhere there was a road that led north to Alaska and in a fleeting thought he could just go and disappear up there.

CHAPTER EIGHTEEN

"Now leaving the United States. Welcome to Canada," were the two signs he had just read in succession as they blurred past the dirty windshield. He slowed the truck to a crawl and then to a halt in front of the customs booth to roll down his window.

The Border Patrol Officer was talking to him through the open window, but he could not make out what he was saying; it seemed staticky, like background noise in his ears. Jack looked straight out through the windshield that was covered with 3,000 miles of sizzling summer dirt and road grime. Robotically he held his license and passport out the window for the officer.

"SIR!" the agent finally said, in a loud and directed fashion to get his attention. "Please answer the question."

Jack turned his blank stare to him, but no words came forth. The officer quickly scanned the disheveled truck inside and out. He saw into the truck cab that was in total disarray, littered with trash, food wrappers and drink cups. The debris covered the dash, seat and floorboard area of the passenger side. It was clear that he was traveling alone because there was no room in the mess for another person to sit.

A waft of air coming from the open truck window greeted the officer's nose. Stale food, sweat, and wet dog, and sure enough there in the backseat of the cab, curled into a ball he saw the source of the last smell, a grey-faced black dog surrounded by bags of gear and a food bowl.

The bed of the truck was covered with a cap, and through the side window the officer saw piles of fishing rods stacked everywhere and what looked like a sleeping area big enough for one person. The officer then turned his attention back to the driver.

Jack still had no answer, nor had he even really heard the generic questions the officer asked of everyone, "What is the purpose of your trip, and how long will you be in Canada?"

The question was still ringing in his ears, when he realized he had not even made eye contact with the agent, for Christ's sake, he had not even blinked. Slowly he turned his head back forward in silence and again stared out through the dirty windshield, looking in the distance for something that was not there.

The words in his head started again, and he glanced briefly at the piece of paper taped to the dashboard of his truck. On it was written "30 DAYS TO DIVINITY." He did not know what the fuck that even meant, where it had come from, or why he had written it down in the first place and had taped it to his dashboard.

For a moment, he stopped to try and think when had he even done it? How long had that been taped there? When had the words started in his head? He could not remember a time when they were not there, like they had come with the truck when he bought it. A yellow Post-It note with Scotch tape around all four sides, so it stayed in place.

No longer yellow and bright, the paper was faded, dirty, and tattered, a brownish color now like a fall leaf that had not fully turned a brilliant color but had faded to brown and had fallen off the tree. Tattered now, it still contrasted boldly against the black and grey of the dashboard.

The voice inside his head had started again, and was saying the four words incessantly, like on a loop, maddening as it continued without relief. Now was not the time for it; he had to stay out of his head and try to focus on what was real and happening right now in this actual moment.

He had to let go of the unexplainable that had been happening to him for weeks now and focus. The simple fact that Jack realized he had to get out of his head made him smile ever so slightly to himself. There was a time when this mental prison was impossible for him to even recognize, let alone escape from.

The officer was still talking and clearly now losing his patience. He had signaled for a second officer, not a, "all hell is about to break loose," but a glance of eye contact to the officer who floated between the booths just in case this aloof driver turned out to be more than just distracted or reclusive.

The floating officer had arrived on scene and stood directly in front of the hood of the truck on the driver's side corner so that he could hear any verbal exchange between the driver and the booth officer, while acting as a human barrier of sorts in case the driver tried to leave the booth prematurely.

The action of the floater coming to the booth and assuming a defensive posture with the vehicle had automatically put the rest of the officers on alert, and a third officer quickly came up along the passenger side of the truck from the rear.

Guns had not been drawn, yet, but both officers were on high alert, their eyes and ears fixed on Jack in the driver's seat, and their right hands in very close proximity to their holsters. Jack was loudly and forcibly instructed to pull the truck over to the inspection area. He looked up, directly into the eye of the officer in the booth for the first time, blank, cold, and distant, and said, "The dog and I are going fishing."

"Sir, please pull over to the inspection area immediately. Turn the truck off, take the keys out of the ignition, and place them on the dashboard, then put your hands-on top of the steering wheel, and wait for further instructions." This was bellowed back at Jack with no acknowledgement of his prior statement from the officer.

Jack pulled into the designated spot and put the truck in park in the inspection area, shut off the ignition, put the keys on the dash, and his hands on the top of the steering wheel as he had been instructed to do. The officer from the booth was now standing at the driver's side window. There was another officer at the passenger side window and still another directly in front of the hood of the truck.

The officer asked if there were any weapons in the vehicle, Jack thought of the many knives in the front and back of the truck, along with a camping ax and a sledge hammer. He shook his head no, "I have no firearms," he declared, and the officer seemed satisfied with his answer. He then instructed him to get out of the truck slowly and to keep his hands in plain sight.

The sight of three officers surrounding a pickup truck in plain sight of the Customs' booths had garnered everyone's attention and every car that passed the inspection area was filled with staring eyes, prying looks, and open mouths; it was the rubbernecker trifecta.

Jack, who had never had more than a speeding ticket in his life seemed to be completely unaffected by it all, like it happened every day to him. Once out of the truck he was directed to put his hands on the hood and spread his legs so that he could be frisked. As he was being frisked, the officer was still asking him questions. It never dawned on Jack once throughout this whole proceeding as to why this was happening to him, or that he had caused the whole thing to escalate to this level. He simply did not care anymore about the cause or the consequences.

The officer on the passenger side asked if the dog was friendly so that they could remove him and search the cab of the truck.

"Yeah."

The rear passenger side door was opened, and Fin stood there looking quizzical, as if to ask the officer what was going on, and why did he have to get out of his comfy bed?

Jack called, "Fin, here!"

Fin jumped out of the truck and trotted over to Jack's left side. He looked at the people standing around as if to say, "Chill."

As the other two officers started to search the truck cab and bed for any signs of contraband or something unusual, the booth agent continued questioning Jack, asking him again, "What is the purpose of your trip, and how long will you be in Canada?"

Jack answered quickly this time as he had finally started to fully understand and grasp the severity of the situation he found himself in, but he still did not make eye contact as he spoke. "The dog and I are going fishing."

"Where?" the officer interrupted. "Do you have a specific destination and timeframe for your fishing trip?"

"I do not know how long it will take" Jack answered. As the words slipped off his tongue he started hearing, "thirty days to divinity" in his head again over and over. Damn that infuriating message.

"How long will what take?" the Officer quickly asked and thankfully diverted Jack's attention away from the voice in his head. "What *exactly* are your plans?" This time the question was far more insistent. "Where are you going fishing, and is that your ONLY purpose here in British Columbia?"

Jack had answered him truthfully already. He said he was going fishing and he also said he did not know for how long. He knew he had slipped up when he had said he did not know how long it would take, but that was also truthful, because Jack had no fucking clue where he was even going, what he was looking for, let alone how long it would take to find it, whatever the hell IT was.

"IT" had dragged him over 3,000 miles, chasing the sunset every day as he drove west. "IT" had been gnawing at him his whole life, the pull to the west, the watching of each day's fading sun on the horizon, and the wondering where it was going, the constant questioning of what else was beyond what he saw? "IT" had brought him to this place, in this very moment, talking to border patrol, being questioned, and about to be arrested if he were not careful.

The booth agent again interrupted Jack's internal monologue, "Jackson Straw, please answer, or we will put you under arrest."

Hearing his own name, "Jack Straw," momentarily yanked Jack back to reality. Most people didn't get it right away, or ever, he thought. His mom had named him after a fictitious character in a Grateful Dead song when she discovered she was pregnant shortly after a torrid affair following one of their concerts in the summer of 1970. Jack himself never knew the real story behind his name until he was in his forties.

This Jack Straw was not from Wichita at all, but a sleepy little town nestled on the eastern shore of Lake Ontario in upstate New York. His head momentarily cleared, and Jack cut him off with no sense of urgency.

"The dog and I are going to the Skeena River, steelhead fishing; I figure I have enough supplies for about thirty days in the truck. When they run out, I assume I will head home. Those are my plans."

Jack looked the officer square in the eyes now, and said again, "Those are my plans." The gaze was blank, devoid of any emotion, but there was intent in his eyes.

The other two officers were concluding their search of the cab and gave the signal for, "all clear" as their search had not turned up anything unusual. With that, the officer was satisfied and handed Jack back his passport and driver's license and waved him on.

Fin jumped back up into the cab of the truck, nonchalantly reclaiming his spot. Jack got in, started the truck, and pulled away into another sunset.

CHAPTER NINETEEN

Jack awoke to the sound of moving water outside his truck. The old Dodge had found its way yesterday afternoon after the incident at the border to a quiet dirt road on the banks of the Fraser River.

Unlatching the cap door, he dropped the tailgate down as the sweet scent of running water and fresh breeze filtered through endless pine trees and entered the stuffy enclosed bed of the truck to replace the stale smell of feet, man, and beast. Jack took another full breath of the delicious air and held the inhale deep in his lungs for as long as he could until his body expelled the breath with a gasp.

Watching the antics of his faithful friend who had already exited the bed of the truck, he wondered to himself if Fin were enjoying this new-found gypsy life, or did he wonder why they were in someplace new every day. The thought was fleeting as it clearly looked like Fin was enjoying himself as Jack soon heard a splash signaling, he had found the river and was swimming already.

The morning air was warmer than Jack had imagined and standing there shirtless at the back of the truck was still a viable option for the moment, but he estimated in his mind that today might be the last day of t-shirt and shorts weather for the rest of the trip because the further north he went into the mountains, the temperatures and the weather would be drastically different.

Jack got dressed and headed off in the direction of the river bank to look around and see where his wandering friend had gone. There in the shallows was the black dog, pretending he was a grizzly bear, chasing spawning salmon in every direction. Fins, tails, and salmon heads were visible and then gone into the obscurity of the murky currents in a blink as their pursuer closed in.

Fin had found hundreds of new playmates and he wasn't going to waste the opportunity to frolic with them. The shenanigans lasted twenty minutes and produced such folly that Jack's sides hurt from laughing so hard.

Excited at the prospect of a heavy tug and bent rod, Jack corralled the salmon chaser, headed back to the truck, and in short order was in the parking lot of a tackle shop. The switch had been flipped inside him after seeing those salmon and he was in full blown fishing mode now. He had unknowingly made a pilgrimage to the Mecca of the Steelhead and Salmon fishing world.

Jack had daydreamed about the picturesque settings that awaited him, huge snow-covered mountains looming like a guardian angel, rivers teeming with fish following their ancient ancestral path instinctively from the ocean up the rivers of their birth.

Jack whispered to himself, "I only wish my Gramp were here to share this with me."

With that statement Jack's whole demeanor once again changed as sorrow and regret flooded his heart as it ached again for their companionship and comradery. Jack stopped browsing immediately as the grey cloud he had just created obscured the morning sun he had been basking in and he hastily found the counter where they sold fishing licenses.

As he approached, the clerk looked up and greeted Jack, "What can I do for you, sir?"

"I need a non-resident fishing license please."

"What you need is a swift kick in the ass, and to remember what you have learned and to finally start putting it into practice."

Jack was only half listening to the clerk until he realized it wasn't the clerk's voice anymore. He snapped his eyes up and there in front of him, wearing the clerk's shirt, with a wide smile and a name tag that said "STU" was the familiar face of his friend.

"What the hell are you doing here?" Jack proclaimed as he blinked twice in order to make sure what he was seeing was really what he was seeing.

"I'm here Jack because *you don't listen!* You must enjoy wallowing in grief, sorrow, and guilt because you put yourself in that position repeatedly."

Jack hung his head at Stu's words as he tried to formulate a response to his assumption, but he couldn't come up with anything. He knew Stu was right, and he knew the lessons he was referring to. In Montana, Stu said Gramp would never miss out on an epic fishing trip just because he was physically gone. Then in the backseat of the truck and at the lake he had reiterated that he was never alone unless he chose to be.

Feeling empowered suddenly, he looked up at Stu and said, "You're right."

"Right about what, sir?" the clerk – the real clerk - asked as he held out the license.

"Nothing, sorry, I was talking in my head." Jack took the license and the regulations book from the clerk's hand and thanked him for his help.

CHAPTER TWENTY

Jack woke the next morning and through the cap windows could clearly see that it was light out and the instant sound of rain on the cap told the remainder of the story. He quickly slid his warm uncovered body out of the sleeping bag and into the chilly air inside the enclosed bed of the truck. "So much for still being warmed by my summer sun," he mumbled to himself while pulling on his clothes.

His feet hit the ground with a splash as he jumped down straight into a puddle, and Fin followed him with a secondary splash of his own. Each of his exhales were now visible in the morning air that was no more than forty damp degrees. Jack headed down to the river to check conditions as the rain fell like a cow pissing on a flat rock.

With every passing minute the outlook of fishing today was dwindling away. A certain level of anxiety was tickling Jack in the back of the throat about not being able to fish today and he had to consciously acknowledge to himself that if it did not happen today, he had all the time in the world now to wait for a day when he could.

That internal acknowledgement made him feel better and put him at ease. There was, in fact, no ticking clock on this trip or his life right now. He did not have to be anywhere at any time in the future, so he forced himself to relax about it.

It was not a far drive until Jack came into a town. As the rain had not let up, he figured he would treat himself by stopping at a diner for a late breakfast. "Finally, my appetite has returned," he said to himself, "Jack, we are going to go have a nice meal and relax on a rainy day, ok?"

"Okay" he replied to himself, and in the door, he walked.

Once inside he took the last remaining empty seat at the counter. It was almost eleven a.m. and he was not sure whether to look at the breakfast or lunch menu. When the waitress approached with a pot of coffee, he asked what was currently being served.

"Whatever you like, honey," as she flashed a flirty smile at him, "breakfast is anytime, and it is late enough now for lunch too." Impressively, she poured the coffee into the cup, didn't break eye contact, and never spilled a drop. "Do you know what you want?"

"Yes, I'll take a short stack of pancakes with Canadian bacon since I am in Canada and all," he said to her with a wry smile on his face, "and I will also have the special I saw when I walked in, the hot turkey sandwich with gravy and mashed potatoes."

The waitress laughed, "jeez, Darlin, are you expecting an army?"

"Nope, just one starving soldier today, ma'am."

At the same time the man sitting to his right at the counter chimed in, "By the way, up here in Canada, we just call it bacon, eh."

Jack was caught off guard by the interjection of sarcasm aimed at his joke to the waitress and before he judged its intent he turned to his right and made eye contact with the source. He took a sip of the scalding hot coffee which burned when it touched his upper lip. He promptly put the cup down and looked annoyingly to see who the smart-ass was. There was Stu's smiling face looking back at him.

Everyone in earshot of the commotion paused to look at him as Jack took a sip of ice water to cool down his scorched lip.

"So, you're a ghost or an angel, which is it?"

"I already told you what I am that morning on the river, do you remember?"

Jack had to really think about that question, as many times as he had replayed all of those events, he must have missed this answer. "No sir, I don't remember."

"I'm the guide that you asked for."

"Yes, yes, I remember now, you said you were the guide I asked for five seconds before you showed up, but I meant a fishing guide. What kind of guide are you?"

"Well, our first meeting didn't go so well so I figured I better wait until you called for me to show up again, and I am glad I did because our time together in Montana was very beneficial to you."

Jack surveyed his surroundings as the occupants of the diner were moving about like normal, but the waitress hadn't been back over to him in a while and no one had looked their way since Stu started talking.

"Are you real, Stu?"

"You've watched me cast a fly line and eat a steak, does that seem real to you?"

"Am I the only one that can see you?"

"Normally, yes, but I allowed Dave to see me that morning, so he could validate me and make you stop thinking you were crazy and had made it all up."

"Did God send you to me?"

"Just like heaven, God has many names. Only human beings care what you call it, but every name is correct if that's what you feel."

"Why me?"

"Because you need help and you asked for it."

"Then why did you disappear on me? We were having such a good time, it hurt to be alone again after that."

"You are no less alone when you can see me, then when you can't, if you have chosen to feel that way. Feel connected and be connected, no matter where you are or what you can see."

Absorbing what Stu had just said, Jack could feel his words resonate deeply inside of him. He shook his head gently in agreement as he looked back to his plate and took another bite. His thoughts were calm and accepting, filled with belief and possibility.

Jack had formulated his next question as he finished chewing and turned back to Stu to ask it. He touched his arm to get his attention and when the face looked at him it was someone else. Stu was gone.

"You said to the waitress since you are in Canada, which must mean you are not from Canada, eh?"

Jack stared for a moment at the man's face as he spoke, putting all the pieces of the puzzle together and bringing himself up to speed very quickly so as to not look strange. Jack realized this man is who made the joke and the whole conversation with Stu had just taken place inside that moment in time between this man's words and Jack's response. The soldier immediately pressed on without a blink.

"No sir, I'm not from Canada. I'm only passing through on my way to Alaska," Jack answered with a laugh at his bacon joke, "I wanted to do a little fishing along the way in your beautiful Province as I made my way north, except this monsoon temporarily halted those plans this morning. I'm specifically chasing Steelhead."

With that declaration the stranger sitting next to him opened up a flood gate of knowledge and experience of this area which he bestowed it upon Jack. Hurriedly he took notes on a napkin, writing everything down so no detail would be missed or forgotten later.

By now, Jack had eaten a quarter of his gravy covered sandwich and mashed potatoes when his stomach finally told his eyes that they were in fact *bigger* than it was.

He had the waitress box it all for him, and excitedly Jack knew later at some point tonight that would be his dinner. Jack paid his bill as he was frantically writing all the details he had just been told on three napkins.

"Thank you, sir," as Jack reached out his hand toward the man, "your knowledge of the area and your willingness to share it with a stranger is wonderful and I am grateful. My name is Jack, pleasure to meet you," He stood now to leave, reaching his right hand across his body while the man looked at him and gave him a nod of acknowledgement for the compliment he had just been paid.

"You're very welcome, and best of luck on your trip."

Jack waited for the waitress to return with his three individually boxed items that she had put into a plastic bag for him and had tied the handles into a knot, so nothing would spill or tip over. Jack thanked her repeatedly as he got up from his seat and made his way to the door.

CHAPTER TWENTY-ONE

Jack woke up and turned over on his bed roll to face the ferocious beast with the black fur and huge white fangs and extended his arm as far as he could reach until he was able to feel the soft grey muzzle.

He began to rub and scratch it like the beast liked, all the while asking him repeatedly if he was a good boy. This playful banter was quickly misinterpreted by the beast who wiggled his way down from his penthouse bedroom to the lower level where he was trying desperately to get as close to him as possible. Jack laughed heartily from deep within his belly as the ferocious beast had morphed into a slobbery, snuggly, lovey, fuzz ball who only wanted play time and lovin's from his best friend.

Soon what started out as a pet, then turned into a snuggle fest, had now become a full-fledged battle royal, steel cage death match complete with snarling fangs, profanities, and insults about the four-legged creatures' mother being a pink poodle.

Jack studied the grey fur on Fin's muzzle. Fin's getting older, flitted through his head, but he cleared those thoughts away.

"Alright, fuck-face!" Jack said to Fin as he playfully cuffed him in the back of the head, "Get up and let's get this day moving already and enough with the grab-assing around!" Fin instantly thought this sneak attack was a prelude to round two and he nipped at Jack's hand that had just cuffed him.

"I said knock it off," as Jack grabbed the dog's face with both hands and held it, so he can look directly in his eyes when he said it again, "Knock it off I said!"

He released the beast and rolled over onto all fours and opened the cap and tailgate, "Go pee." In a flash, the sleek, jet black menace was out and going about his business.

CHAPTER TWENTY-TWO

Jack was shaking his head in disbelief as he glanced down over the side of the bridge to the water below. His friend from the diner had failed to mention that the bridge was one lane and still partially made of wood. "I must be in God's country."

Looking downstream from the bridge the currents were slick and glassy and the continual upwelling gave them the appearance of softly boiling water in deep shades of blue, green, and aqua. "If your soul was thirsty," Jack thought, "and needed to be quenched, then this would be the water that you drank."

Jack had the impression that if he dipped his hands into the water, he could pull out a chunk of it and look at it, glistening in his hand like translucent gelatin that was a part of the whole organism as opposed to flowing with loose relation to the other molecules. It appeared to him, in an instant, to be the fishiest water that he had ever seen, and his excitement for this float trip was soaring through the roof as he hurried back to the truck.

His plan was simple, load his dry bag with gear for today, tonight and tomorrow, float and fish the five or six miles downstream to where the river went back along the highway. When he reached that spot tomorrow evening then he would ditch his gear on the bank and walk the distance back to his truck.

This was uncharted water and he had no idea what it was going to be like until he was in it. There was no hesitation or trepidation inside of him what so ever. He chose not to feel alone and disconnected, and it was working. This felt to Jack like a culminating moment in his life and he was visualizing how it was going to play out in his mind.

Jack had read about a concept called mindfulness and how **it was a matter of slowing yourself so that you are acutely aware of yourself and your surroundings in the moment and not disconnected and removed from yourself and your life, basically, be an active participant in your life instead of a bystander watching things happen.**

Part of the building excitement about this adventure was the fact that there was no backup, no "Plan B", no one to rescue him if things went south. Self-reliance had been Jack's forte his whole life, and this trip was going to put his life's work into practice.

The inner tour guide in Jack's head was cut off in mid-explanation as his attention was being captivated by the sheer beauty his eyes were seeing downstream.

"Fuck it", he said, "let's go, God hates a coward," and with that rallying cry he pushed off from shore and with the oars paddle him and Fin out into the rolling, boiling aqua colored current. The tiny raft had floated less than a mile from where he had started when Jack heard the audible roar of crashing water in front of him.

The decision to portage his raft was agreed upon in his head as soon as he saw the size and force of the rapids making the noise where two rivers joined. Jack made the portage in one trip and sat down on a rock on the shore to look over the water and to take a break after getting the pack off of his back. He removed his hat and fished around inside the sweat band until he found the object of his affection, a half-burned joint.

The sound of the lighter was the only thing mechanical in this landscape, and the rolling paper singeing as the cherry is stoked by his inhalation to a glowing red an inch from his lips, was as loud as thunder when it was the sole pinpoint focus. As he sequestered the smoke into his lungs, he looked up from the tip of his nose to watch the currents dance in front of him in all directions until movement on the far bank of the river ripped his attention away.

Jack focused two hundred yards away on the far shoreline to see if what had caught his eye was real, and if it would return. There was nothing to see up or down the shore, then in a blink, there was a lumbering leg and then another, upstream and in the brush from where he originally thought he had seen it. Into the clearing where the staircase waterfalls careened down the rocks stepped the enormity of a bear, wrapped in heavy, luxurious, shining, milk chocolate colored fur.

Seconds later a second bear stepped out of the brush along the river bank and into plain view, this one was half the size, and Jack immediately knew he was looking at a Mother and Cub, probably an older Cub, but still a Cub. Years of watching nature documentaries made Jack acutely aware of what he was seeing and rule number one in life was never piss off or threaten a mother while she was with her child, no matter what species they were.

The rush of seeing something like that in the wild with his own eyes was the most thrilling and exhilarating feeling of his life.

CHAPTER TWENTY-THREE

In the fading light of late afternoon Jack surveyed the water before he went about the chore of making camp. "As soon as I wake tomorrow morning, I am going to fish that pocket as the sun makes its way up into the Eastern sky." With one more long look over the water he turned and started to make camp on the little rise in the edge of the trees.

The small tent was set up to protect from the heavy mist that had been falling all day, which could turn to full blown rain at any second, and a modest fire quickly started to warm their damp bones and keep any curious critters away in the night. Dinner for both of them tonight was dry food only, kibble for Fin and two protein bars and a bag of trail mix for Jack who did not dare to cook anything while in Bear country.

Jack stoked the fire before turning in and put a small pile of sticks next to the tent so that if he woke up in the night, he could put them on the fire easily and not have to go searching for the wood. Then he grabbed his bear spray and put it right next to his side so that it was quick and easy to find if something large and furry with big teeth and claws wandered too close in the night.

Nestled in his nylon tent Jack had a moment to reflect on recent events and the boat he had watched on the Mississippi River came to mind, recalling how hard it struggled against the current. They were a deterrent to themselves and to the current at the same time. That boat mucked up the works big time. Maybe that was why the image had stayed with Jack and stuck out to him like it had.

Stu also referenced that boat when they were fishing, and Jack was struggling so badly, he had said to "Get out of my own way, stop being a deterrent to my own current." Jack surmised he must have meant that his mind was the boat and that casting the fly rod was his current. "My mind was getting in the way of casting, which I clearly know how to do, but the mind, my mind, was acting as a deterrent. Do I know what deterrent really means?" So, he pulled out his phone, looked it up, and read the definition aloud.

"The word deterrent means a thing that discourages or is intended to discourage someone from doing something. Deterrence is an act or process that prevents something from happening. So, the boat was the deterrent, the thing that was discouraging the current from flowing freely as it is intended to do, and the person driving the boat was the deterrence. He was committing the act of purposely trying to keep the current from flowing naturally."

"Holy shit, is that right?" And down came the vibrations rumbling through Jack's entire body. He had made sense of the puzzle. The question he had posed, he had answered. Both of those words are rooted in negatives, Jack thought. "I've had enough negatives. What words are the opposite of the negative, what words mean the same thing, but in a positive, uplifting way?"

Jack found the antonyms for deterrent in the online dictionary, and they were words like catalyst, incentive, encouragement, and assistance, but none of those words seemed to fit in with Jack's train of thought on this.

"It makes sense to me that if we have a word for negative things and actions that we should also have a word that means doing or being something positive." Jack was blown away by the words he had just used to describe the thoughts that were flowing through him.

"At any point during that first afternoon in Montana, had I cared enough about myself, to have been patient and loving inwardly, I would have allowed myself and my new fly rod to have fulfilled their true purpose. Sadly, I did not care about, or love, either thing and the horrible frustration, anger, and hate that I felt took over and hurt me deeply. A simple positive thought could have stopped all that negativity in its tracks."

Jack was spent from these revelations, emotionally drained, again feeling like the top of his head had been unscrewed and he was wide open to the universe around him.

Jack paused in his thoughts, speaking aloud again, "What did I say that seemed to resonate just now?" Jack started to retrace his mental steps to see if the trigger would show itself again. Something clicked, "What was it", Jack asked himself repeatedly. "I was talking about food and my mom being a terrible cook and about how thankful I am for having had my grandparents in my life as a boy, how I am forever indebted to them, and boom there it is. Why is the word indebted lighting up for me?"

Jack pulled out his phone and looked up the word indebted. The definition was owing gratitude for something. That seemed right; I owe them gratitude for loving me and raising me, but I already knew that.

His mind was fully engaged now and focused on the screen. What about the prefix "in?" The dictionary listed it as Latin derived and meaning to encompass and/or to have a positive force. Jack immediately knew that meant something.

The boat from the Mississippi River came back in his mind as he remembered the words "deterrent to the current."

Jack looked up from the phone screen at Fin who was curled in a ball next to him. I need to write this stuff down to make sense of it all, and he reached into his backpack and pulled out a small leather-bound notebook.

Jack quickly jotted down the definitions he just looked up. As he wrote the definition of deterrent in his book, he saw the word discourage in the definition and immediately realized he was looking for something that meant the opposite.

If the opposite of discourage is encourage, then what was the opposite of deterrent? Both of those words have negative connotations and prefixes.

"So," Jack said aloud as he wrote furiously in his notebook "if I change the prefix from negative to positive, I would have the word 'interrent' and that would be the opposite meaning of the word "deterrent".

The new word's meaning would be a thing that encourages someone or is intended to encourage someone to do something positive and for their own good.

"No more would there be a deterrent to the current, it would be interrent to the natural flow." The vibrations that had mysteriously expressed yes answers for the last three weeks rang loudly inside of Jack, thunderous, uplifting, and awe inspiring, like bells in a cathedral. "What have I just uncovered Finny?"

"Stu said to '**be patient with myself, to give myself a break, and to love myself before I would be capable of doing that for anyone else.'** This word was exactly what he was describing to me!" Jack turned back to his phone and google searched the word he had just come up with to see if there was a different or conflicting definition that he was unaware of. The screen read 'no results for this search' so he went to the dictionary site and searched the word in there. No results found matching Interrent.

"Did I just make up a new word that didn't exist in the English language?" Yes, came the vibrational answer. Jack had put down his notebook and was staring at the dark starless sky. "Don't be a deterrent, be Interrent." This powerful new phrase kept repeating in his head as the hours of night passed quickly and uneventfully after his revelation.

Sleep had always come quickly for Jack as soon as he laid his head down, and tonight was no different. Never once did he or Fin wake, and somewhere in the pre-dawn Jack began to dream.

He saw the run of pocket water outside the tent, deep opaque green hued water that looked so inviting. He could feel his arms casting as the fly made its way to its intended target.

He saw the large silver flash of the fish as it breached the shimmering surface in the first rays of mornings light. The strain of the fish on his arms made Jack roll from side to side as he slept. Wrestling with something greater than he had ever known.

Looking down the brightly colored fly line and into the depths of the shimmering emerald waters in his dream, he knew that he was looking straight into eternity. Peaceful exuberance combined into a cocktail that was shaken to incorporate both parts. The fish relented and came ashore where Jack handled him quickly and respectfully and soon cradled him as he hoisted his trophy of a lifetime.

CHAPTER TWENTY-FOUR

Jack was up and out early. He made twenty drifts with the wet fly in the first pocket without a touch. He grabbed his fly, cut it off with his teeth, put it back in its box and reached for the dry fly box where he found a pattern tied from the Trey Combs penned bible, "Steelhead Fly-fishing."

"I think this is going to be the ticket." He picked up the fly as soon as it landed and made his first mend as the fly started to wake, when the silver serpent appeared out of nowhere inhaling the fly in an instant. Instinct made Jack's right arm cock at the elbow as he raised the rod sharply in order to drive home the size two barbless hook into the behemoths jaw.

"That was just like in my dream," Jack yelled, as Moby Steelhead hurled himself out of the water careening downstream, "Christ sakes that's a big fish," he then blurted after seeing what looked to be a forty plus inch fish clear the glistening surface of the water like a missile.

"Calm yourself," he said, "do what you know how to do. Be Interrent." The heavy surge in the rod, and then a limp feeling that the change of direction had caused, had Jack reeling as if his life depended on it. He caught up the slack line and was again tight on the fish.

"This is the greatest fight of my life," Jack continued to narrate the action. "This is what I have journeyed so far and so long for."

The fight soon subsided as Jack and fish were both exhausted. He kneeled in the water to unhook and admire his catch. He cradled the fish and looked to his companion as he always did to show him what he had caught. Fin was not returning his master's gaze though; he was looking back to where the tent was and the campfire that still smoked slightly.

Jack followed his gaze and there standing before him were the three kings, illuminated in the morning sun and shining like beacons across eternity. Jack instinctively recoiled from being startled, and then just as quickly he softened as he saw Stu's familiar face. "There is someone here I'd like you to meet, my boy."

Next to Stu in the middle of the three men and standing noticeably taller than the other two with his huge left hand extended and his gangly thumb sticking straight up in the air with approval was the man who had loved him and raised him and was his whole world, his beautiful Grandfather. The smile of pride on his face made Jack explode inside with the warmth of a watch fire.

Jack was drawn to the face of the third man whom he did not recognize but was unable to look away from. The face was kind and familiar with dark eyes and hair like his own whose smile lit up his face as genuine as he had ever seen. Jack could only stare as he started to examine the features that looked undeniably similar to his own.

The question came from inside of Jack without warning as it passed over his lips and into the air, "Are you my father?" The words hung in place like the clouds of mist that had been overhead for days.

The answer came as the fish in Jack's hands jerked violently causing him to look down at it. When he did, the fish made eye contact with him, clearly, and without a shadow of a doubt, and said yes with his eye and then stayed motionless in his hands.

Jack stared as he lowered the fish back into the water and pointed his head upstream, amazed in his realization that none of this had been about the coveted size of this fish or the fishing at all. It had all been a pathway to this moment. The fish of his lifetime rendered insignificant in a moment by the sight he had always dreamed of seeing.

Still kneeling Jack turned back to the firepit where the men were standing but they were gone. He scanned in every direction in case they had moved, but in his heart, he knew they were gone. Tears of joy poured down his cheeks as he did not make a sound until he stood up and said, "You came back for me, Dad. After all these years of wondering who you were, where you were, you have been with me all along, haven't you?" and the bells of heaven rang out the answer in Jack's ears.

"Are you still alive?"

"Yes," whispered through the trees.

A song started to play in his head, a lilting, bouncing little upbeat ditty. He knew the tune, but it took a moment to catch up when it suddenly came into focus.

"I'll tell you where the four winds dwell. In Franklin's tower there hangs a bell." Franklin's tower sent ripples through Jack's soul as the music in his head continued, "It can ring, turn night to day. It can ring like fire when you lose your way!" Instantly Jack knew the name that had eluded him his whole life.

"You're Franklin," as he paused to clear his throat, "aren't you?"

"Yes."

Jack's mind was blown. "Where do you live? How will I ever find you?" there was no answer to the improperly formatted question and Jack scrambled to reword his frantic thoughts. "Do you live on the east coast?"

No answer.

"Do you live on the west coast?"

"Yes."

"British Columbia?" Jack thought suddenly that it would make sense if he were here for a reason, but there was no response.

"Washington?"

"Oregon?"

"California?"

"Yes."

Holy shit, Jack thought, *he's in California, I'm turning around and head south immediately.*

"Do you want me to find you?" There were no bells, or vibrations this time, just the words clearly whispered in Jack's ear.

"Yes."

"Thirty days to divinity" flashed across his mind from out of nowhere as Jack bent down to pick up his fly rod.

"I'm not finished yet, am I?" The bells rang their response and Jack hustled to break camp and get back to the truck. Once in the driver's seat he yelled into the backseat where the dog was lying, "Hang on tight, boy, we're headed back to the border."

CHAPTER TWENTY-FIVE

Jack had ample time to think and reflect on what had just taken place as he drove south back down the sparsely populated highway that he had just traversed two days prior. Conspicuously gone now was the unrelenting feeling of searching for something and not knowing what that something was.

"How could I have ever thought that catching a fish, even a once in a lifetime fish, would bring me eternal peace and happiness? That's an external thing, a possession, a conquest, an ego driven thought that if I could do this thing, then and only then I would be complete, whole, happy, or satisfied."

"Once all of those conditions that I set were met, "I thought" only then would the happiness pour over me and my life would forever be bliss, but that's not how this works at all."

"Should I keep myself unhappy, unfulfilled, unappreciated and unloved?" And again, there was no answer.

He had never felt he deserved love before now; he felt unlovable because his father had abandoned him, and Jack had allowed that feeling of abandonment to curse his life. Seeing his father today changed that thinking just like he had changed directions on this trip. He allowed himself to see his value and worth that were present all along.

The suffering he had endured all his life as after effects of these feelings were self-induced and were not true or in his best and highest good in any way. This all seemed so clear now, but it hadn't always been that way.

"I stumbled upon the idea of loving myself enough to embrace and act in a fashion that is in my best and highest good," Jack said aloud as he drove, "I was even able to come up with a word to describe the feeling, not out of coincidence, but in preparation for what just transpired."

"I feel like I am listening and paying full attention for the first time in my life, and I have been rewarded for it by seeing the three men who are most dear to me, or at least most dear to me now. I have awakened limitless possibilities."

Jack pondered what he had just said. His gramp had been in his life since he had been born and had held the highest place if one were to rank. Stu quickly became influential and a true teacher but was more than that. The lightbulb went off.

"He is my guide, my spirit guide, right?" The truck suddenly shook and vibrated as if he was driving on the rumble strips. The answer was yes, a dramatic yes. "I knew it!" Jack blurted with a smile on his face.

"How did I know the third man was my father though? How could I have known?" Jack knew he was asking the question in the wrong format to receive an answer, but it was the first thing that popped into his mind.

Jack reached his arm behind his seat as he drove, trying to find the warm fur of his traveling companion, giving him a quick rub to wake him up as they were approaching a town where they could stop, refuel, stretch, pee and anything else two men might do after driving for seven straight hours.

Jack's hand found its intended target scratching Fins head and snout briefly and with unusually little response in return. As he pulled his hand away, it brushed over the tip of his nose that was noticeably warm and dry. Jack dismissed it as being cooped up in a warm truck for hours.

"Can I please have three cheeseburgers, two orders of fries, a large root beer float and an ice water?" to the voice on the other end who read back his order which Jack acknowledged.

"I am going to walk my dog while the food is being made, so I will leave the window rolled down for you to put the tray on if I am not there when you deliver it."

The voice on the other end of the speaker came back obviously young and seemingly confused, "Umm, okay."

Jack chuckled to himself at the confusion he must have just caused but he figured they would be able to sort it out somehow and still deliver the food, even to an empty truck.

He got out and opened the back door to grab Fin's leash and put it on him. When he looked up to grab his collar, Fin was still laying down on his bed which again was unusual. Jack placed his hands on either side of the dog's face and looked him in his glassy, sleepy looking eyes.

"Are you ok, bubby?" he asked. Fin's tail wagged slightly as he blinked. "Come on now, don't play possum on me; go potty and let's get something to eat."

The dog wobbled to his feet, jumped down from the cab of the truck and gingerly walked to the grass on the side of the building. Once away from traffic and people, Jack unhooked the leash and let Fin roam about.

Jack grabbed his food bowl and unwrapped one of the cheeseburgers, pouring fries over the top of it. His furry buddy was going to destroy this meal as burgers and fries were his favorite.

Jack put the bowl down on the ground and filled the water bowl with the ice water and setting that next to the food bowl which he instantly noticed the dog had barely touched.

"What the fuck is going on with you, Finny?" Jack asked him, "Are you not feeling well?"

Fin wagged his tail at Jack in response as if to say everything was all right; he took a few bites and lapped slowly at his water bowl. Jack, on the other hand, had no problem eating and polishing off his two burgers and fries in short order while washing it down with his float.

"All right, mutt, if you're not going to eat then let's get back in the truck and keep moving."

Driving in the dark was monotonous, and his mind wandered to and fro between the beginning of this journey to where he found himself now. It amazed him what the last month had shown and taught him, with sights and experiences truly beyond comprehension.

Looking back, he saw how hard he had fought what was unknown, and now he was purposely driving straight toward it. He looked down at the dirty yellow Post-It note taped to the dash of the truck just above the radio that said three twenty-four in the morning.

"I have been driving seven hours, and by the looks again of the gas gauge I need to find a place to fill up soon. Considering that I have not seen or passed another car in hours, I do not want to be stranded out here."

He pulled into the twenty-four-hour gas station that surprised him for being in such a remote area simply called One Hundred Fifty-Mile House. He was sure there was an interesting story of how the tiny town got its name, but for now, he needed to fuel up, piss, and get the dog out for a quick walk.

Jack opened the door and Fin barely looked up at him, which again was an unusual sign for him, but he shrugged it off as a lazy old dog who was being harassed to go out in the cold night and pee on command. Jack grabbed his collar and pulled him down out of the truck.

Fin stumbled when his feet hit the ground and there was a slight arch to his back as he walked. Jack had never seen this before, but now gave it his full attention. Fin soon lifted his leg to pee, but it was barely off the ground and he pissed all over the leg which was still in the line of fire.

"What the hell is going on, boy?" Jack demanded of the dog like he should be able to answer him and tell him what the problem was.

Now, back at the truck Fin tried to jump in the cab and didn't make it high enough. He fell backwards into Jack who caught him in his arms before he hit the ground. He looked up at Jack as if to say, "Please help me get in my bed."

Jack cradled him under the belly and gently lifted him into the truck. He left the door open and ran around to the driver's seat where he retrieved his phone and Googled 'Vets near me.' The listing came back with two names of mobile clinics, but they were not near this area and the third listing was for "Divinity Animal Kingdom" in Devine, B.C., four hours away.

CHAPTER TWENTY-SIX

Arriving at the Clinic he wasted no time in scooping the seventy-five-pound animal into his arms. Jack reached the front door and freed up one hand briefly to pull it open, but it was locked.

"Fuck", he yelled as he realized even though the lights were on they were not open for business yet. He could no longer wait, so he began to kick the door in lieu of knocking since his hands were full of dog. He kicked hard enough to be heard. Within seconds the latch was undone, and the door flung open.

"Doc," Jack blurted, "my boy is sick and now unresponsive, and I don't know why."

He followed the Vet down the hallway to an examination room. "It started yesterday afternoon when we came off the river and has gotten worse over the last eighteen hours as we drove south. When I pulled in here just now he wouldn't wake up."

Jack laid Fin on the exam table and continued to rub his head and talk to him softly as the vet took his vitals.

"Please, Doc," Jack begged as he looked up for the first time to see two brilliant green eyes looking back at him.

"Has he had anything to eat or drink since you noticed this?"

"No," Jack answered. "We stopped last night, and I got him his favorite, burger and fries, but he only ate two fries and drank a little sip of water."

"Ok," she said. "Go out and have a seat in the waiting room while I get started."

"No," Jack replied, "I'm not leaving him."

"Sir, I need you to let me do my job. Please go out to the waiting room."

Jack reached down and kissed Fin on his motionless head and begrudgingly exited the room. As he walked down the hall he heard someone come in the front door and looked up to see a vet tech dressed in brightly-colored scrubs looking quizzically at him and why he was there as they passed.

"The doc is in the back with my dog." The tech nodded and quickly walked past him as he watched her open the exam room door and could hear the two of them talking as the door shut.

Jack found a seat in the waiting room as the minutes turned to hours. How could this be happening to him again, he thought. After the death of his grandparents he had sworn to never allow himself to be close to anyone for fear of losing them and going through this terrible pain, but the years had turned Fin into his family, and now that family was on the verge of being ripped apart.

"I thought I had more time with him," Jack kept repeating to himself as he sat there alone. "Why is this happening, and for what reason? This trip has been teaching me that it's okay to let go, that there is no such thing as gone in the universe, *BUT,* I don't want to be alone here without my best friend."

"And, where is Stu when I need him the most? I need a guide now and he's nowhere to be found. Why doesn't he pop in like he always does and startle me, and tell me what to do and how to act, or to remember a lesson or an answer that I already know? And what about this new word I discovered, *Interrent,* where are its positive forces that are supposed to make everything alright? All of these things that have been happening to me are bullshit if they disappear when they are really needed."

His eyes became heavy, as the crippling fear he felt had turned to rage and drained him to the point of exhaustion. At some point, he dozed off sitting upright in the waiting room chair. There was no peace in this sleep and the dream of Fin standing next to gramp in the lush green field had turned into a dark and barren landscape. Jack knew in his unconscious state that it meant Fin had died. He felt his chest tighten as he tried to scream and break free from the darkened dream world, but to no avail.

Frantically he tried to wake himself from inside the dream, thrashing his arms and legs as if trying to escape an invisible captor. The shaking of his shoulder felt like rumble strips on the white line as he opened his bloodshot, burning eyes to see who was standing in front of him.

She smiled brightly at him out of habit, not joy, "Sir, it's ok, you must have been having a dream, you're awake now, I'm Dr. Courtney Freehold. I'd like to talk to you about Fin."

Jack's reserve battery did its best to kick in and make him alert enough to comprehend what she was saying.

"Would you follow me to my office, so we can talk in private?" she said as she reached out her hand to help him up.

"Why in *private*?" Jack blurted out as panic suddenly returned like in the dream and filled his voice. "Oh my God! Is Finny boy dead? I told you he was all I had! How could you let him die!"

Jack's body went limp as he slid forward out of the chair crashing to his knees, lifelessly hunched over. Hands covering his face, he began to sob uncontrollably over the loss of his best friend.

Without warning Jack's fight or flight instinct kicked in to hyper drive as adrenaline got him to his feet and he bolted for the door.

"Sir COME BACK!" the vet screamed as she tried to grab his arm as he fled.

The blank grey sky and ice-cold rain slammed him in the face like a fist and stopped him in his track's half way down the sidewalk. He stood motionless, wet hair matted against his face as streams of tears and rain ran down his cheeks. There, fifteen feet in front of him, stood his guide, Stu, dry and calm.

"Listen to me, boy, When the storms rage and the rains come, that is when you need to have the deepest belief and faith. It is NOT the time to throw away your umbrella."

Reality blurred in the moments that followed until he felt arms wrapped around him as tightly as he had ever felt before. The sound of a softly whispering female voice in his ear reassuring him that Fin was not dead and that everything was going to be all right, brought a halt to the waves of fear crashing onto his shore.

Dr. Courtney loosened her embrace and ushered Jack quickly back inside. Jack raised his head to look into her eyes as she stood before him. She placed her hands on either side of his face, held them tight and said, "I don't know what is wrong with him yet, or if he'll make it, but you have my word that I will do everything in my power for you both."

Jack muttered incoherently, "He's all I have," still processing what Stu just said to him.

"Sir, are you listening to what I am telling you?"

"Yes," inattentively peeped across his lips.

"We're going to have to keep him here and monitor him for a while. Go home and I will call you as soon as I know more."

"My home is parked out in your parking lot."

"Come with me then," as she reached out her hand for him, "there are some dry clothes in my office and a couch where you can lie down, I'll wake you when there is news."

Jack went this time without resistance and lay in the darkened office. He stared unblinkingly at the wall over the desk. There, the name of the business was written exactly like the sign in the parking lot. Jack read the words silently as vibrations tingled his entire body. Flabbergasted by what he was reading and putting the jumbled puzzle pieces together as best he could, Jack began to count the days on the calendar of his phone.

Tomorrow is day thirty since I started on this trip and I'm sitting here in Divinity Animal Hospital, "30 days to divinity!" Just like the words taped to the dashboard. "I can't believe this is happening. Is this where I was supposed to be all along?" The vibrations rang out their response. "But why?" he asked, "what is here for me?" and there was no answer.

Exhaustion had gripped Jack; the severity of Fin's condition had stripped him of any remaining resistance, and his head hung down toward his chest. With his final effort Jack opened the umbrella over his head, shielding himself from the rain. "I accept whatever happens here as being what is best for me, I have faith, I believe." His eyes were already closed as he spoke, and his breathing relaxed easily into a sleeping rhythm.

Immediately he was back in the dream of his Gramp standing in the field calling for Fin who was running to meet him. It looked peaceful and serene as he watched them both. Jack then heard his voice calling to Fin, begging him to come back, telling him it was not his time yet.

The dream built to a fevered pitch as he called and called to Fin like he was lost. Then suddenly, Jack sat up from a dead sleep as a cold, wet nose was pressed against his cheek, followed by a slobbery dog tongue that washed the entire side of his face in one motion. Eyes opened and instantly cleared, and the shining black furry face looked back at him while the whipping tail went a hundred miles an hour.

"FIIINNNNNNNNN!!!!!!!!!" Jack screamed with delight as the tail wagging mass of black fur danced around on his tip toes sharing in Jack's excitement over their reunion.

"YOU CAME BACK!" as he squeezed him around the neck as tightly as he can. "I'm so happy, I thought you left me." Quickly Jack turned to Dr. Courtney standing in the doorway. "What happened, what was wrong with him?"

"I really can't answer that, we gave him a shot of antibiotics and some IV fluid with no response, then he just woke up like this a few minutes ago looking around for you like you were calling him."

"I was calling him, in my dream just now, I was calling him to come back home and he did."

Jack slid off the couch and onto the office floor petting and hugging Fin as Courtney came and knelt beside them. "Thank you, thank you, thank you," is all Jack could say as he continued to hug and pet Fin.

"You're very welcome, sir."

"Don't call me sir, I work for a living," he said with a wry smile, "call me Jack, Jack Straw."

With a grin and a delicious giggle, she responded, "Let me guess, you're from Wichita?"

Shocked that she knew the reference of his name, he focused solely on her now that he could think straight. He watched her mouth as it moved and noticed that it was framed by the most perfectly-formed lips he had ever seen. Unconsciously he wondered what they would feel like pressed against his.

That thought caught him off guard as he had never thought that way about a stranger before under any circumstances, and he was not an impetuous man by any means, especially when it came to romantic feelings. He briefly thought it was a reaction to the joy he now felt after being so distraught over Fin's condition.

The emotions continued to overwhelm Jack as he couldn't stop his eyes from scanning her hauntingly familiar features. Kneeling there in front of him, she shone like the sun, her face illuminated and framed by her long chestnut-colored locks that were pulled into a tail and then clipped to the top of her head. She was beauty personified, pure, simple, and genuine.

Jack was spinning as if intoxicated, and the déjà vu feeling that he knew her, was overwhelming as it hammered at his mind like the fist of an intruder at the front door. Courtney got up off her knees and walked toward her desk as Jack stared at her movements, studying every step and sway of her hips. Her gait looked so familiar to him, yet he was drawing a blank, and then it popped like a bursting water pipe dousing everything around it.

"Holy fuck, it's *HER*!" he hissed to himself as a flood washed over him like a scalding hot shower when you first stepped into it, stinging and inviting at the same time. A state of disbelief drowned Jack as he was mentally transported back to the lakeshore where he had watched the same sultry walk and swaying hips coming toward him in his erotic fantasy.

He felt the blood immediately start to course through his veins, as the sight of her on the beach undressing as she walked toward him in his fantasy replayed in his mind. "What is happening to me; focus for Christ's sake and stop staring at her like a middle school boy ogling a high school girl on the bus, you weirdo."

"Did you say something Jack?" she said as she sat down at her desk so as to not interrupt the reunion.

Jack rose and walked directly over to her at the desk. Their eyes fixed on each other now as he arrived. "I have so much to say to you that I don't even know where to start. I barely know you but feel like I already do."

"I'm getting the same feeling," as she flashed him a bright smile. "You're going to think I'm crazy when I tell you this but I'm going to anyway. One of my clients that I see from time to time has come in twice in the last month with his parrot saying it was sick. I haven't found anything wrong with it and I've started to assume he's just a lonely older man who wants someone to talk to now and then. It's fine because we end up sitting and talking and I truly love our visits as he is a very kind man. I've never heard him mention a wife or family, but he always asks how I am doing and how my love life is."

This perked Jack up and with fingers crossed he nonchalantly asks, "I*s* there anyone in your life?"

"No, there isn't, but this is the funny part of the story. Yesterday when Stu, that's my client's name, brought in the bird who strangely he calls gramp for a checkup, it kept repeating to me, *"He's coming!"* and when I questioned Stu about it, he said he'd never heard the bird say that before. Then he added with a devilish grin that maybe "gramp" knew something he didn't. Then you show up this morning pounding on my door."

The color left Jack's face in an instant as he began to shake his head slowly from side to side.

"Jack, is everything ok?"

"Yes, it is," he said with a smile, "I have a very dear friend named Stu as well, and I'm absolutely sure that he is overjoyed that you saved Fin and that we've had a chance to meet."

"What a coincidence we both know someone with a rather uncommon name like Stu."

"There are no coincidences Doc, and when I tell you the rest of the amazing story that brought me here to you, you'll agree." Without hesitation he hugged her and kissed her on the cheek as he whispered in her ear, "Thank you for saving my best friend and me."

The Dr. returned his embrace and said, "You're very welcome." As they parted, she paused; now nose to nose with Jack their eyes met. Delicately she moved forward tilting her head slightly to the side and kissed him passionately.

When their lips finally separated Jack saw her face was flushed as she waited to see his response. "I don't know what's come over me, I've never…."

Stopping her with a finger across her lips he whispered, "It's ok, in fact it's a million times better than ok, I've been waiting for you my whole life."

Courtney looked at Jack and brushed her hand on his cheek, "Me too, I now know it's been your face I've seen since I was three years old. I've kissed your lips and slept in your arms a thousand times in my dreams. I left my home in New Jersey years ago and wound up here for reasons I never knew. Now I know it's because I was looking for something, looking for you. I always knew you were coming, but I didn't know when until the bird told me yesterday, and here you are."

The kiss rekindled as Jack slid his hand behind the nape of her neck to draw her closer, and their future together flashed in front of his eyes like the credits of a movie. The images took Jack's breath away as their lips finally parted.

Inches separated them as they locked eyes and smiled, looking into and through each other. Jack told her without a moment of trepidation, "We've kissed before you know, on the beach at the lake, just a couple of weeks ago. I saw you, felt you touch me, as clearly as I do right now." Jack's words hovered silently in the air above the office.

"That's not all we've done," they both said in unison as they both burst out in raucous laughter that was joined by a barking black dog who wanted in on the group hug.

Jack looked down at his loyal friend, rubbed his head, and said, "We're finally home, boy."

Jack and Courtney's journey continues in the next book coming soon. Stay tuned to the Author's website www.theawakeningangler.com for more details. You can also take the quiz at www.theawakeningganglerquiz.com

CPSIA information can be obtained
at www.ICGtesting.com
Printed in the USA
FSHW022157190120
66205FS